WUJI
FEIJINSHU
JIANZHUCAILIAO
ZHUANYE YINGYU

无机非金属

建筑材料专业英语

黄德馨　金玉杰　主　编
肖力光　　　　主　审

化学工业出版社
·北京·

本书共分四部分。第一部分为基础知识，包括三个单元，介绍了专业英语的基本特点、翻译方法和技巧、科技论文写作的基本知识。第二部分为精读课文，选编了英文文献 12 篇，内容涉及无机非金属材料工程的各个方面。第三部分选编了 8 篇英文文献作为辅助阅读材料。第四部分汇编了混凝土科学方面的专业术语词汇，便于读者查阅。

　　本书针对性强，选材广泛，难度适中，有利于学生提高英语阅读能力和掌握专业知识。本书可供高等院校无机非金属材料工程专业或建筑材料专业师生使用，亦可作为广大从事建筑工程专业工作并具备一定英语基础的工程技术人员及自学者参考使用。

图书在版编目（CIP）数据

无机非金属建筑材料专业英语/黄德馨，金玉杰主编.
北京:化学工业出版社，2011.7
　ISBN 978-7-122-11741-0

　Ⅰ.无… Ⅱ.①黄…②金… Ⅲ.建筑材料：无机非
金属材料-英语-教材　Ⅳ.H31

　中国版本图书馆 CIP 数据核字（2011）第 130256 号

责任编辑：邹　宁　　　　　　　　　　　装帧设计：周　遥
责任校对：周梦华

出版发行：化学工业出版社（北京市东城区青年湖南街 13 号　邮政编码 100011）
印　　刷：北京永鑫印刷有限责任公司
装　　订：三河市万龙印装有限公司
710mm×1000mm　1/16　印张 9¼　字数 208 千字　2011 年 9 月北京第 1 版第 1 次印刷

购书咨询：010-64518888（传真：010-64519686）　　售后服务：010-64518899
网　　址：http://www.cip.com.cn
凡购买本书，如有缺损质量问题，本社销售中心负责调换。

定　　价：25.00 元

前　　言

专业英语是根据大学英语教学大纲的要求设置的基础英语的后续课程,目的是通过专业英语课程的学习,培养学生阅读和翻译英文专业书刊的能力,掌握阅读翻译专业文献资料的质量和速度,熟悉科技论文写作的基本知识,为扩大专业词汇量以及今后学习工作中获取专业信息、掌握学科发展动态、参加国际间学术交流等奠定良好的基础。

编者结合在建筑工程专业英语教学实践中的经验和体会,融合建筑行业的发展状况,专门为高等院校无机非金属材料工程专业(建筑材料方向)学生学习专业英语编写成本书。本书亦可作为广大从事建筑工程专业工作,并具备一定英语基础的工程技术人员及自学者参考使用。

新编教材共分四个部分。第一部分为基础知识,包括三个单元:第一单元,主要介绍专业英语的基本特点;第二单元,专业英语的翻译,阐述专业英语的翻译方法和技巧;第三单元,科技论文的写作,介绍科技英语的基本体例和写作基本知识。第二部分为精读课文。结合专业英语专业性比较强的特点,本部分集中选编了无机非金属材料方面的英文文献12篇,包括基本知识,水泥制造、基本成分及特性,混凝土的基本特性,高性能混凝土,预应力混凝土,外加剂,高性能建筑材料,聚合物改性水泥原理,智能材料,现代建筑及结构材料,陶瓷制造过程,玻璃结构等无机非金属材料工程专业涉及的各个方面的内容。为了给读者进一步学习有关专业英语知识提供方便、进一步扩大本书的知识覆盖面,本书第三部分又选编了8篇文献作为辅助阅读材料。第四部分为词汇表,汇编了混凝土科学方面的主要专业术语词汇,使学习者能准确掌握专业词汇的标准英文表达。

本教材结合学生专业知识学习的特点,英文文献选材针对性较强,选材广泛,难度适中,有利于学生英语阅读能力的提高和专业知识的掌握,并帮助学生通过英语阅读强化所学的专业知识。

本书由吉林建筑工程学院黄德馨、金玉杰主编,钱永梅、王若竹、田伟、钱坤、杨玥、雒峰、谢新颖参编。全书由肖力光教授主审。本书在编写过程中参考了有关文献的部分资料,在此一并表示感谢!

由于水平有限,书中难免有疏漏和不足之处,恳请广大读者和同行、专家批评指正。

编　者
2011 年 7 月

CONTENTS

Part Ⅰ The Basic Knowledge

Unit 1 The Basic Characters of English for Special Purpose

专业英语与普通英语、文学英语相比，有许多独特之处。因为专业英语与专业知识紧密联系，除了包含一些数据（data）、公式（formula）、符号（symbol）、图表（diagram and chart）和程序（procedure）等外，在语言、语法、修辞、词汇、体裁等方面都有其独特之处。下面从语言上、语法上、词汇上和结构上对专业英语的基本特点加以简要介绍。

1.1 The Characters of Language 语言特点

1.1.1 Accuracy 准确

所谓准确，就是要表达准确，要正确理解和分析英语的语法特点与句型，表达上不使用模棱两可的词。从下面的例子，可看出专业英语的语言特点。

【例 1】 The C_3S and C_2S constituents form 70 to 80 percent of all Portland cements,are the most stable and contribute most to the eventual strength and resistance of the concrete to corrosive salts,alkalis and acids.

硅酸三钙和硅酸二钙占各种波特兰水泥熟料组分的 70%～80%，是水泥熟料中最重要的组成部分，因而对混凝土的最终强度及抵抗酸、碱和盐的腐蚀能力起着重要的作用。

1.1.2 Brevity 简洁

专业英语的内容通常包括理论分析、公式推导和研究的目的、范围、方法、步骤、结论等。在不影响表达的前提下，语言应尽可能简洁，避免不必要的润饰和重复。但并不排除会使用复杂句或长句。

【例 2】The rates of heat evolution of the four principal compounds, if equal amounts are considered, would be in the following order: C_3A, C_3S, C_4AF and C_2S.

按等量计算，波特兰水泥熟料中四种主要化合物水化热释放率的大小顺序为：C_3A, C_3S, C_4AF 和 C_2S。

1.1.3 Clarity 清晰

清晰主要是强调逻辑严谨、概念清晰、关系分明、句子连贯等。

【例 3】 The materials are the basic elements of any building. Building materials may be classified into three groups, according to the purposes they are used for. Structural materials are those that hold the building up, keep it rigid, form its outer covering of walls and roof, and divide its interior into rooms. In the second group are materials for the equipment inside the building, such as the plumbing, heating, and lighting systems. Finally, there are materials that are used to protect or decorate the structural materials.

材料是任何建筑的基本元素。根据使用目的，建筑材料被分成三组。结构材料用来支撑建筑物保持其坚固，形成墙和屋面的外部围护以及分隔内部房间。第二组材料是建筑物内部的设备，如垂直运输、加热和提升系统。最后一组是用于保护或装饰的建筑材料。

1.2　The Characters of Grammar　语法特点

1.2.1　非人称的语气和客观的态度，常使用 It…结构

专业英语所涉及的内容多描述客观事物、现象和规律。这一特点决定了科技人员在撰写科技文献时应采用客观和准确的手法陈述被描述对象的特性和规律、研究方法和研究成果等，而不需要突出人。因此，专业英语常常使用非人称的语气做客观的叙述。

【例1】 **It** would seem logical that strong concrete would be more durable, and in many respects, the lower permeability that comes along with higher strength often does improve concrete's resistance to certain durability- related distress, but unlike strength, the prerequisites for durability are not easily defined.

人们常常认为，高强度的混凝土有好的耐久性，在许多方面，低渗透率的高强混凝土可提高混凝土的耐久性，但是与判断强度不同，混凝土的耐久性并不容易评定。

1.2.2　较多使用被动语态

由于专业英语的客观性，决定了它非人称的表达方式。读者或者都知道动作的执行者是谁，或者不需要说明动作的执行者。因此，在专业英语中，较多地使用被动语态。

【例2】 Cements can be divided into 5 categories.

水泥可分为五种类型。

1.2.3　大量使用不定式、动名词、现在分词和过去分词

专业英语中大量使用不定式、动名词、分词，多数情况下是为了使句子简洁和精练。

【例3】 The total weight **being** less, it is possible **to build** much taller buildings.

由于总重量减轻，就有可能建造更高的楼房。

【例4】 A true appreciation of the relevant properties of any material is necessary if a satisfactory product **is to be obtained** and concrete,in the respect,is no different from other materials.

要想获得令人满意的产品，就必须了解所用材料的有关性能。在这方面，混凝土制品与其他材料制品是完全一样的。

1.2.4　较多地使用祈使语气和公式化表达方式

在理论分析和公式推导时常采用 Assume that…，Suppose that…，Let…等祈使语气表达方式。

【例5】 **Suppose** that $P = 0$ at $x = y$.

假定当 $x = y$ 时 $P = 0$。

1.2.5　条件语句较多

条件语句多用于条件论述、理论分析和公式推导中，最常用的是 If…条件句。

【例6】 We also have a pretty detailed understanding of the hydration process and the structure and properties of the hydration products, even if there are a few unsolved questions.

尽管存在一些没有研究透彻的问题，但我们仍然对（水泥的）水化过程以及水化产物

的结构和性能有非常深入的了解。

1.2.6 长句较多，但一般比较简洁清晰

【例7】 An admixture is defined as a material other than water, aggregate, and hydraulic cement, **which** might be added to concrete before or during it's mixing.

混合材料不同于水、骨料及水泥，它有可能在拌和混凝土过程中加入，也有可能在拌和之前就已加入。

例句中，关系代词 **which** 引导定语从句，在从句中作主语。

1.2.7 省略句较多

为了简洁，有时省略掉句子中的一些部分，如状语从句中的主语和谓语、定语从句中的关联词 which 或 that，从句中的助动词等，但基本不省略形容词、副词。

【例8】 **If not well managed**, the procedure for construction may be more expensive.

如果管理不善，这一施工方法还可能造价更高。

常见的省略句型有：

As already discussed	前已讨论	If possible	如果可能的话
As described above	如前所述	If so	倘若如此
As explained before	前已解释	When(If) necessary	必要时
As indicated in Fig.1	如图 1 所示	When needed	需要时
As previously mentioned	前已述及	Where feasible	在实际可行的场合
Where possible	在可能的情况下		

1.3 The Characters of Words and Expressions 词汇特点

1.3.1 专业 (Special) 词汇和半专业 (Semispecial) 词汇

每个专业都有一定数量的专业词汇或术语。例如，对建筑材料专业，有 cement（水泥）、concrete（混凝土）、masonry（砌块）、sulphate（硫酸盐）、air entraining agent（引气剂）、gypsum（石膏）、lime（石灰）等；对高分子材料，有 polymer（聚合物）、butadiene（丁二烯）、monomer（单体）、polyethylene（聚乙烯）、viscosity（黏度）等。

专业文献中的专业词汇一般有三类。第一类是纯专业词汇，它的意义很单纯，只有一种专业含义，有时候则是根据需要造出来的，如 fire-proof brick（耐火砖）、prestressed concrete（预应力混凝土）等。第二类是半专业词汇。它大多是各个专业通用的，在不同的专业领域却可能有不同的含义。如：foundation（基础、基金、创立）、frame（框架、屋架、机座、体系等）、operation（操作、运行、作业、效果等）、load（荷载、加载、装入、输入等）。第三类是非专业词汇。这类词汇是指在非专业英语中使用不多，但却严格属于非专业英语性质的词汇。如：application（应用、用途、作用、申请等）、implementation（实现、执行、运行）、to yield（产生、得出、发出等）等。

1.3.2 词性 (Syntactical Functions) 转换

专业英语也较多使用了词性的转换。转换后词意往往与原来的词意相关。常见的词性转换类型有：名词→动词、形容词→动词、动词→名词、形容词→名词等。这里有两种情况，一种是词本身可以在句子中充当另一种词类；另一种是在译文中被转换成另一种词类（参见 Part Ⅰ.Unit2）。例如：standard（n. 标准）→standardize（v. 标准化）;former（adj.

3

前面的）→the former（*n.*前者）;wide（*adj.*宽的）→widen（*v.* 加宽）。

1.3.3　词缀（Affix）和词根（Etyma）

由于历史的原因，英语中的很多文字源于外来语，如希腊语、拉丁语、法语、德语、意大利语和西班牙语等。有些词是日常生活中常用的，例如 economical, immigrate, foreword 等；有的则用于某些专门的领域。例如在土木工程领域，有 hydraulics, infrastructure, reliability, specification 等。据有关专家统计，现代专业科技英语中，有 50%以上的词汇源于希腊语、拉丁语等外来语，而这些外来语词汇构成的一个主要特征就是广泛使用词缀（包括前缀 Prefix 和后缀 Suffix）和词根。因此，如果适当掌握一些词缀和词根，就有助于扩大词汇量。

1.3.4　缩写（Abbreviation）、数学符号（Mathematical Symbol）及其表达式（Expression）

在阅读和撰写专业文献时，常常会遇到一些专有词汇或术语、物理量等单位的缩写，或一些政府机构、学术团体、科技期刊和文献等的简称。举例如下。

Fig.（Figure）—— 图

Eq.（Equation）—— 方程（式）

m/s（meter/second）—— 米/秒

in.（inch）—— 英寸

Eng.（Engineering）—— 工程

i.e.（拉丁语 *id est*）——也就是，即

etc.（拉丁语 *et cetera*）—— 等等

psi.（pounds per square inch）—— 磅/英寸

Sym.（Symmetry or Symmetrical）—— 对称

QC（Quality Control）—— 质量控制

CAD（Computer Aided Design）—— 计算机辅助设计

RILEM（International Union of Testing and Research Laboratories for Materials and Structures）—— 国际材料与结构试验研究所联合会

CIB（International Council for Building Research Studies and Documentation）—— 国际建筑研究及文献委员会

FIP（International Federation of Prestressing）—— 国际预应力混凝土委员会

FIB（International Federation for Structural Concrete）—— 国际结构混凝土联合会

ISO（International Organization for Standardization）—— 国际标准化组织

ECCS（European Convention of Constructional Steelworks）—— 欧洲钢结构学会

ASCE（American Society of Civil Engineers）—— 美国土木工程师学会

ICE（Institute of Civil Engineers）——（英）土木工程师学会

CSCE（Canadian Society for Civil Engineering）—— 加拿大土木工程学会

ACI（American Concrete Institute）—— 美国混凝土学会

ASTM（American Society for Testing & Materials）—— 美国材料与试验学会

EI（Engineering Index）——（美）工程索引

1.4　The Characters of Structure　结构特点

上述语言、语法和词汇特点属于专业英语"语域分析"的内容。这些内容形成了专业英语的基础。更进一步，还需要了解专业英语在段落及文章层面上的结构特点，了解隐含在语言运用中的逻辑思维过程。这样，才有助于把握文章的要点和重点，提高阅读和理解能力。

一般在每一自然段落中，总有一个语句概括出该段落的重点。这个语句或在段落之首，或在段落之尾，较少出现在段落中间。若干个自然段落会形成一个逻辑（或结构）段落，用以从不同角度来解说某一层面的核心内容。全篇则由若干个逻辑段落组成，从不同层面来阐述文章标题所表明的中心思想。

仔细阅读下面一篇短文（其中包括对土木工程的一些重要特性的说明），分析其结构特点，并结合前面提到的语言、语法和词汇的特点，进一步体会专业英语的特点。

Polymer-modified Mortar and Concrete

① Polymer-modified mortar and concrete are prepared by mixing either a polymer or monomer in a dispersed, powdery, or liquid form with fresh cement mortar and concrete mixtures, and subsequently curing, and if necessary.

② Several types of polymer-modified mortars and concretes, i.e., latex-redispersible polymer powder-, water-soluble polymer-, liquid resin-,and monomer-modified mortars and concretes, are produced by using the polymers and monomers. Of these, the latex-modified mortar and concrete are by far the most widely used cement modifiers.

③ Although polymers and monomers in any form such as latexes,water-soluble polymers, liquid resins, and monomets are used in cement composites such as mortar and concrete, it is very important that both cement hydration and polymer phase formation (coalescence of polymer particles and the polymerization of monomers) proceed well to yield a monolithic matrix phase with a network structure in which the hydrated cement phase and polymer phase interpenetrate. In the polymer-modified mortar and concrete structures, aggregates are bound by such a co-matrixphase, resulting in the superior properties of polymer-modified mortar and concrete compared to conventional.

...

上面三段是选自某一课文的前 3 个自然段，这 3 个自然段叙述的是聚合物改性砂浆和混凝土。

第一段为一句话，介绍了聚合物改性混凝土的制备方法。可以看出，语句无任何修饰成分，用非常简洁的语言介绍了聚合物改性砂浆和混凝土的制备方法。第二段为两句话，说明了聚合物砂浆的分类。第三段阐述了制备聚合物改性砂浆和混凝土材料的关键所在，指出除去聚合物外，水泥的水化与聚合物的性能对聚合物改性砂浆和混凝土的制备亦相当重要。

这三个自然段的重点就是聚合物改性砂浆和混凝土，全文的逻辑关系是：preparation-classification-key factors，逻辑性强，从不同层面来阐述文章标题所表明的中心思想——聚合物改性砂浆和混凝土。

Unit 2　The Translation of English for Special Purpose

2.1　Introduction 引言

所谓翻译，就是把一种语言文字的意义用另一种语言文字准确、完整地表达出来。从这个意义上讲，它是使用不同民族的语言交流思想的工具，也是一个复杂的思维过程，包括观察、记忆、理解、分析、综合、联想、判断、选择等多种思维活动，是另一种语言文字对原作的思想、氛围、风格进行的一次再创造。

专业英语是英语的一部分，但它又具有独特的形式及专用语言。一般来说，在掌握了一定的英语基础之后，人人都可以动手翻译，但译文未必能满足专业人员的要求。因此，专业英语的翻译就要求翻译者在英语、汉语和专业知识等方面都具有良好的素质和修养。真正地掌握专业英语的翻译，应该主要从以下几个方面着手：

① 掌握适当的专业词汇以及专业符号等；

② 学会分析句子结构（尤其是复杂句）及文章结构，透彻体会原文思想；

③ 学会运用适当的翻译方法和技巧，在忠实原文的基础上，按照汉语的习惯及专业习惯等将原文准确地表达出来。

2.1.1　Standards of Translation 翻译的标准

翻译的任务在于准确而完整地介绍原文的思想内容，使读者对原文的思想内容有正确的理解。要解决这个问题，就需要有一个共同遵守的翻译标准来衡量译文的质量，来指导翻译的实践。因此翻译标准是衡量译文质量的尺度，又是翻译实践所遵循的原则。

对于翻译的标准，一个比较统一的观点是：信、达（或顺）、雅。"信"是指准确、忠实原作；"达"是通达、顺畅；"雅"是文字优美、高雅。由于专业英语本身注重表现技术问题的科学性、逻辑性、正确性和严密性，所以，专业英语的翻译标准更侧重于"信"和"达"。

【例 1】 The importance of good performance building material can not be overestimated in the realm of construction.

直译为：在建筑领域中，性能优异的建筑材料的重要性不能过分估计。

应译为：在建筑领域中，性能优异的建筑材料的重要性无论怎么估计也不过分。

在原文中，over 这种复合词在与 can not 连用时相当于 can not…too…，表示"无论如何…也不过分"。直译显然误解了英语的这种特有的表达方式。英语中有许多词存在这样的情况，这是翻译中必须注意的问题。

【例 2】 Today's concretes are in general less durable than the "old" (pre-1960) concretes.

直译为：　通常，今天的混凝土比"旧"混凝土的耐久性差。

应译为：现代混凝土的耐久性不及以前的混凝土耐久性好。

从以上两个译例可以看到，翻译一定要在准确透彻理解原文的基础上才能进行，切不可不求甚解，想当然而译之。"信"对翻译而言极其重要。然而，"达"是指译文的语言形式应该符合汉语的规范，即翻译时要考虑到汉语的行文习惯和表达方式。译文不顺主要表现在语句的欧化上，逐字死译、生搬硬套。

2.1.2 Process of Translation 翻译的过程

翻译的过程是正确理解原文和创造性地用另一种语言再现原文的过程，大致可分为阅读理解、汉语表达和检查校核等阶段。

（1）阅读理解

阅读理解阶段是翻译过程的第一步，也是重要的阶段。阅读理解主要是通过联系上下文、结合专业背景进行的。通常应注意两个方面：一是正确地理解原文的词汇含义、句法结构和习惯用法；二是要准确地理解原文的逻辑关系。

【例3】 Concrete is too often mistreated during its placing and curing, so that in the field, an excellent concrete can be instantaneously transformed into a poor concrete.

直译为：在混凝土的养护过程中，如果经常不注意养护，那么在某种程度上，好的混凝土也会变成贫混凝土。

应译为：在混凝土的养护过程中，如果经常不注意养护，那么在某种程度上，优质的混凝土也会变成劣质混凝土。

good 译为"好的"，意思上固然不错，但不符合专业术语行文的习惯，应改译为"优质的"方为妥当。poor 译为"穷的"在这里显然是不行的，应改译为"劣质的"。由此可见，在选择词义时，必须从上下文联系中去理解词义，从专业内容上去判断词义。

（2）汉语表达

表达阶段的任务就是译者根据其对原文的理解，使用汉语的语言形式恰如其分地表达原作的内容。在表达阶段最重要的是表达手段的选择，同一个句子的翻译可能有好几种不同的译法，但在质量上往往会有高低之分。试比较下面的译例。

【例4】 Tremendous advancements in the scientific understanding of the physics of metals, dielectrics, and semiconductors has taken place.

译文一：在科学理解金属、绝缘体与非金属上取得了巨大的进步。

译文二：人们在对金属、绝缘体与非金属的科学理解上取得了巨大的进步。

译文一语言不够简练通顺；译文二完全摆脱了原文形式的束缚，使译文准确贴切，简洁有力。

（3）检查校核

理解和表达都不是一次完成的，往往是逐步深入，最后达到完全理解和准确表达原文的内容。因此，在翻译初稿完成之后，需反复仔细校对原文和译文，尽可能避免漏译、误译。

【例5】 Theoretically, it may be used for either statically determinate or indeterminate structures, although for practical purposes the method is limited to determinate structures because its use requires that the stress resultants be known throughout the structure.

理论上，这个方法既可用于静定结构，又可用于非静定结构，但在实际应用中，它只限于静定结构，因为用这种方法时，要求知道整个结构的应力合力。

翻译时，既要分析句子的结构，又要考虑逻辑关系，同时要保证没有漏译或误译的现象。由此可见，校核对翻译而言也是非常重要的，尤其在专业英语翻译中，要求高度准确，其中的术语、公式、数字较多，稍有不慎就会造成谬误。

2.2　Contrast between English and Chinese　英汉语言对比

在翻译中，进行英汉两种语言的对比是十分重要的，特别是比较两者的相异之处。通过对比，能够较为准确地掌握各自不同的特点，这对具体的翻译实践大有帮助。

2.2.1　Contrast of Words and Phrases　词汇的对比

英汉词汇的对比主要是从英语的词义、词的搭配和词序来比较其在汉语中的对应情况，看其对应的程度，以及具体使用时会发生怎样的变化。

（1）词义方面

英语词汇意义在汉语里的对应情况，大致有四种情况。

① 词汇意义一一对应，即对于一些已有通用译名的专有名词和术语等，英汉词汇的意义完全相同。如：civil engineering 土木工程（学）；flexible foundation 柔性基础。

② 英语词汇意义比汉语更广，如：material — 比汉语"材料"意义更广；straight — 比汉语"笔直"意义更广。

在这种情况下，英语中的词汇与汉语中的词汇在词义上只有部分对应，在意义上概括的范围有广义与狭义之分。例如，material 一词还有物质、剂、用具、内容、素材、资料等词义。翻译时，对这类词要仔细掂量、认真推敲。

③ 英语词汇意义不及汉语广，如：road — 不及汉语的"道路"的意义广；car — 不及汉语的"汽车"意义广。

这种情况正好与第二种情况相反，例如，中文中"汽车"一词泛指公路车辆，而 car 一词则专指轿车。

④ 英语词汇与相应汉语词汇部分对应，两者的意义都有彼此不能覆盖的部分，如：book 书；state 国家；do 做。

这种情况在英语和汉语词汇关系中是最普遍的，而且也是最难处理的，所以翻译时特别要注意。

从以上列举的四种情况可以看出，翻译绝不是填充，绝不能用某一固定的汉语词去填充某一固定的英语词。一个词的具体意义，只有联系上下文才能确定，如果离开了上下文，孤立地译一个词就很难确切地表达该词的真正含义。

（2）词的搭配

英语和汉语在词的搭配能力方面往往有差异。如 reduce 基本词义是"减少"，但其搭配范围很广，翻译时需酌情选择适当的汉语词汇。例如：

reduce to powder	粉碎
reduce the temperature	降低温度
reduce the time	缩短时间
reduce the scale of construction	缩小工程规模
reduce the numbers of traffic accidents	减少交通事故

英语中一个词可能会有很多意义，翻译时需要注意按汉语的习惯合理选择相应的搭配。

【例 1】 Two or more computers can also be operated together to <u>improve</u> performance or system reliability.

可同时操作两台及以上的计算机，以<u>改善</u>其性能或<u>提高</u>系统的可靠性。

（3）词序方面

英语和汉语句子中的主语、谓语、宾语和表语的词序大体上是一致的，而定语和状语的位置则有同有异，变化较多。

① 定语的位置　英语中单词作定语时，通常位于所修饰的名词前，但也有少数单词要求后置。汉语的单词作定语一般都前置。如：

<u>movable</u> span	活动跨
<u>journey</u> speed	运行速度
something <u>important</u>	重要的事情

英语中短语作定语一般位于所修饰的名词之后，汉语通常需要前置，间或也有后置的情况，主要看汉语的习惯。如：

| a building project <u>of tall apartment houses</u> | 高层公寓大楼的建筑项目 |
| one <u>of the common</u> defects in concrete maintenance | 混凝土维修中普遍存在的问题之一 |

② 状语的位置　英语中单词作状语，其位置有三种情况：修饰形容词或其他状语时要前置；修饰动词时可前置也可后置；表示程度的状语在修饰状语时通常前置，但也有后置的情况，在汉语中状语一般都需前置。

英语中短语状语可放在被修饰的动词之前或之后，甚至可插入情态动词（或助动词）与实义动词之间。译成汉语时，通常需放在所修饰的动词之前，但也有后置的情况，这要视汉语的习惯而定。

【例2】　It is only natural that hydraulic cement concrete would be viewed as a single material, <u>but in reality</u>, concrete is much better understood when viewed as a composite material comprised of two fundamentally different materials—filler (i.e. aggregate) and binder (i.e. paste).

通常，人们将水泥混凝土看作是单一材料，<u>但事实上</u>，将混凝土理解为由填料（即骨料）和黏结料（即黏结剂）组成的复合材料更好一些。

【例3】<u>To the extent possible,</u> the foundation concrete is placed keeping the excavation dry.

<u>应尽可能</u>在保持基坑干燥的情况下灌筑基础混凝土。

2.2.2　Contrast of Syntax　句法的对比

英汉句法对比主要是指句子结构和句序的比较分析。

（1）句子结构

英语和汉语在句法结构上有许多不同之处，因而，表达一个相同的意思所运用的表现手法也不尽相同。英语常常使用各种连词、关系代词和关系副词来表达分句以及主句与从句之间的各种关系。而汉语则主要借助词序以及词与短语之间的内在逻辑关系来连接并列复合句和偏正复合句。英译汉时虽然在有些情况下不需要转换句子结构，但很多情况却必须进行这种转换。英汉句子结构转换大致有以下五种情况。

① 英语简单句结构转换成汉语复合句结构

【例4】　Considered from this point of view, the question will be of great importance.

如果从这点考虑，这个问题就十分重要。（英语简单句——→汉语偏正复合句的假设句）

② 英语复合句结构转换成汉语简单句结构

【例5】 Water power stations are always built <u>where</u> there are very great falls.

水力发电站总是建在落差很大的地方。（英语状语从句──→汉语简单句）

【例6】 It is essential <u>that</u> material science students have a good knowledge of chemistry.

学材料科学的学生掌握化学知识是极为重要的。（英语主语从句──→汉语简单句）

③ 英语复合句结构转换成汉语不同的复合句结构

【例7】 Tents are still used by necessity by some nomads or by modern people who want to experience the type of life our ancestors lived.

翻译：那些流浪汉或者是想体验我们祖先生活的现代人会用帐篷。

④ 英语的倒装句转换成汉语正常句序　在英语里，倒装主要是考虑到上下文或语气上的需要，以突出中心。汉语一般不用倒装结构，故英译汉时常常需作适当改变。

【例8】 Only in this way can we obtian a high performance cocnrete.

只有这样我们才能获得高性能混凝土。

⑤ 英语被动结构转换成汉语主动结构，反之亦然

【例9】 Concrete is too often mistreated during its placing and curing, so that in the field, an excellent concrete can be instantaneously transformed into a poor concrete.

在混凝土的养护过程中，如果不经常注意养护，那么在某种程度上，优质混凝土也会变成劣质混凝土。

（2）句序

句序是指复合句中主句和从句的顺序。英语和汉语的句序对比实际上就是比较英语复合句和汉语复合句中按时间和逻辑关系叙述的顺序。

① 时间顺序　英语复合句中，表示时间的从句可以置于主句之前或之后，叙述顺序很灵活，汉语则按照发生的时间顺序叙述，而且汉语的时间通常位于句首。

【例10】 In the year 2000, more than 1.5 billion tonnes of cement were produced to make, on average, nearly 1 cubic metre of concrete per capita.

2000 年水泥产量超过 15 亿吨，相当于平均每人使用 1 立方米混凝土。

英语复合句中有时包含两个以上的时间从句，各个时间从句的次序也比较灵活，汉语则通常按照事情发生的先后安排其位置。

② 逻辑顺序　英语复合句若是表示因果关系或条件与结果关系，其叙述顺序比较灵活，原因从句或条件从句可以位于主句之前或之后，而汉语中大多是原因或条件在前，结果在后。

【例11】 Normally, the latex-modified mortar and concrete require a different curing method because of the incorporation of polymer latexes.

通常，由于存在聚合物乳液的聚合过程，聚合物改性砂浆和混凝土的养护方式（与普通混凝土）不同。

2.3　Selecting and Extending the Meaning of a Word　词义选择及引申

在翻译时，经常会出现一个英语单词对应多个汉语意思，或某些词在词典上找不到适

当的词义，难以确切表达原意，甚至造成误解。所以，应根据上下文和逻辑关系，选择恰当的词义，或从其基本含义出发，进一步加以引申。

2.3.1 Selecting the Meaning of a Word 词义的选择

现代英语中，一词多类、一词多意的现象特别普遍。同一个词往往属于几个词类，具有不同的意思。因此，在翻译时，需要准确的选择词义，引伸词义，还要注意词类的转译问题。

（1）与词的语法特征有关

① 词性不同，词义有别

【例1】 Using prestress to eliminate cracking means that the entire cross section (rather than the smaller cracked section) is available to resist to bending.

利用预应力来避免裂缝的出现意味着整个截面（而不是开裂后的较小截面）可以抗弯。（prestress 作名词）

【例2】 When a curved tendon is used to prestress a beam, additional normal force develops between the tendon and the concrete because of the curvature of the tendon axis.

当采用曲线钢筋束来对梁施加预应力时，由于预应力钢筋束轴线的弯曲影响，在钢筋和混凝土之间会产生附加径向压力。（presstress 作动词）

② 名词单复数、可数与不可数引起词义改变

【例3】 As a result of those economies, many of our most important new projects in other fields became possible.

由于采取了这些节约措施，我们在其他方面的许多最重要的新工程才得以实施。

economy 单数形式既可作"经济"、"经济制度"解，又可作"节约"解，但复数形式则是指具体的"节约"措施，不能译为"经济"。

③ 普通名词与抽象名词意义的转变

【例4】 Beijing was the first permanent settlement.

北京是最早的永久性居住地。（settlement 用作普通名词）

【例5】 Enormous stretches of arable land in the central western region are still awaiting settlement.

中西部地区还有大片可耕地有待于垦拓。（settlement 用作抽象名词）

（2）与词的搭配有关

同一个词、同一类词在不同场合具有不同含义，必须根据上下文的联系及词的搭配关系或专业知识来理解和确定词义。

【例6】 The works of these watches are all home-produced and wear well.

这些表的机件均系国产，耐磨性好。

【例7】 Bridges are among the most important, and often the most spectacular, of all civil engineering works.

桥梁是土木工程建筑中最为重要的一种，也往往是最为壮观的一种。

（3）与汉语表达有关

【例8】 The gears work smoothly.

齿轮运转灵活。

【例 9】 Statesmen have always <u>worked</u> for peace.

政治家们一直在为和平<u>努力</u>。

2.3.2 Extending the Meaning of a Word 词义的引申

词义引申时，往往可以从词义转译、词义具体化、词义抽象化和词的搭配四个方面来考虑。

（1）词义转译

【例 10】 The choice of material in construction of buildings is basically between steel or concrete, and the main trouble with concrete is that its tensile strength is very <u>small</u>.

钢材和混凝土是建筑施工的基本材料，混凝土的主要缺点是抗拉强度<u>很低</u>。

（2）词义具体化

英译汉时，根据汉语的表达习惯，把原文中某些词义比较笼统的词引伸为词义比较具体的词。

【例 11】 There are many <u>things</u> that should be considered in any experiment.

实验中有许多<u>因素</u>应当考虑。

（3）词义抽象化

英译汉时，有时需要根据汉语的表达习惯把原文中词义比较具体的词引伸为词义比较抽象的词。

【例 12】 We have <u>progressed a long way</u> from the early days of some high performance concrete.

高性能混凝土从出现以来，已经有了<u>很大的发展</u>。

（4）词的搭配

【例 13】 In order to get a large amount of water power, we need a <u>large</u> pressure and a <u>large</u> current.

为了大量的水力，我们需要<u>高的</u>水压和<u>强的</u>水流。

2.4 Method of Changing the Syntactical Functions 词性的转换译法

在翻译的过程中，原文中有些词需要转换词性才能使译文通顺自然。词性转译主要有以下四种情况。

2.4.1 Changing into Verb 转译成动词

同汉语相比，英语句子中大多数只有一个谓语动词，而汉语动词用得比较多。在该使用汉语动词的场合英语往往会用介词、分词、不定式、动名词或是抽象名词等来表达。

（1）介词动词化

许多含有动作意味的介词，如 across、past、toward 等，译汉语时通常转译成动词，一些仅表示时间、地点、方式的介词如 in、at、on 等，虽然没有动作意味，但译汉语时根据汉语的行文习惯有时也需转译成动词。

【例 1】 Mechanical stabilization is still considered <u>of</u> great value in construction of the United States.

在美国施工中，机械稳定法仍然被认为<u>具有</u>很大的价值。

（2）名词动词化

英语中有大量从动词派生的名词和具有动作意味的名词，这类名词在英译汉时常能转译成汉语动词。

【例 2】 This giant entertainment building is under <u>construction</u>.

这座大型娱乐建筑正在<u>兴建</u>。

（3）形容词动词化

英语中表示知觉、感觉、情感、欲望等心理状态的形容词在系动词后作表语时，常常可转译成汉语动词。

【例 3】Steel is widely used in engineering, for its properties are most <u>suitable</u> for construction purposes.

钢材广泛地用于工程中，因为它的性能非常<u>适合</u>于建筑。

（4）副词动词化

英语中有些副词本身含有动作意味，例如：on, back, off, in, behind, over, out 等。这些副词在英译汉时往往需译成动词。

【例 4】 An exhibition of new building materials is <u>on</u> there.

那里正在<u>举办</u>新型建筑材料的展览会。

2.4.2 Changing into Noun 转译成名词

（1）动词名词化

英语中有很多名词派生的动词和由名词转用的动词，在英译汉时不易找到适当的汉语对应词，因而常将其转译成汉语的名词。

【例 5】 These cracks, however, must <u>be</u> closely <u>watched</u>, for they <u>are</u> constantly <u>being attacked</u> by unfavorable environments.

由于<u>经常受到</u>不利环境因素的<u>侵蚀</u>，这些裂缝必须<u>加以</u>密切<u>观察</u>。

（2）形容词名词化

英语形容词转译成名词大致有三种情况：一是有些形容词加上定冠词表示某一类人或事，汉译时可译成名词，如 the rich（富人），the poor（穷人）等；二是英语的关系形容词在汉语里没有对等词，汉译时常作名词处理，如 ideal structure（理想结构）等；三是科技英语中往往习惯用形容词来表示物质的特性，汉语却习惯用名词，通常在这类形容词后加上"度"、"性"等词而转换为汉语名词。

【例 6】 Of those stresses the <u>former</u> is compressive stress and the <u>latter</u> is tensile stress.

在两种应力当中，<u>前者</u>是压应力，<u>后者</u>是拉应力。

（3）副词名词化

英语中由名词派生的副词时常可译成名词，少数不是名词派生的副词有时也可译成名词。

【例 7】 Structural drawings must be <u>dimensionally</u> correct.

结构图的<u>尺寸</u>必须准确。

2.4.3 Changing into Adjective 转译成形容词

（1）名词形容词化

形容词派生的名词，及带有不定冠词或介词 of 作表语的抽象名词在汉译时可以译成形容词。

【例 8】 The methods of prestressing a structure show considerable <u>variety</u>.

对结构施加预应力的方法是<u>多种多样</u>的。

【例9】 This experiment is an absolute <u>necessity</u> in determining the best water-cement ratio.

对确定最佳水灰比而言，这次实验是绝对<u>必需</u>的。

（2）副词形容词化

当英语动词或形容词汉译时名词化后，修饰该动词或形容词的副词也会相应形容词化。

【例10】 It is a fact that no structural material is <u>perfectly</u> elastic.

事实上，没有一种结构材料是<u>完全的</u>弹性体。

2.4.4　Changing into Adverb　转译成副词

（1）名词副词化

【例11】 We find <u>difficulty</u> in solving this problem.

我们觉得<u>难以</u>解决这个问题。

（2）形容词副词化

英语名词转译成动词时，修饰名词的形容词自然就转译成副词。另外，由于英汉两种语言的表达习惯不同，英语形容词有时需转译成副词。

【例12】 Scientist have made a <u>careful</u> study of the properties of these material.

科学家们<u>仔细</u>研究了这些新材料的特性。

由于句中词性的转化，相应地产生了句子成分的转换，即原文句子中的某一语法成分（主语、谓语、宾语、表语、定语、状语等）改译成另一种语法成分。

【例13】 <u>Attempts</u> were made to find out measures for reducing the shrinkage of this material.

<u>曾试图</u>找到减小这种材料收缩的措施。（主语转换成谓语）

【例14】 The test results are <u>in good agreement</u> with those obtained by theoretical deduction.

试验结果与理论推导者<u>完全一致</u>。（表语转换成谓语）

2.5　Methods of Adding and Omitting　增译和省译法

翻译时对原文内容不应该做任何删节或增补。但由于两种语言的表达方式不同，把原文信息译成译文信息时，常常需要删减或增添一些词。这样做并不损害原意，反而可以使译文更为通顺，意思更为清楚。这种省略和增补不仅是许可的，而且常常被看成是一种翻译的技巧。

2.5.1　Methods of Adding　增译法

增译法是在翻译时根据句法上、意义上或修辞上的需要增加一些无其形而有其意的词，以便能更加忠实通顺地表达原文的思想内容。当然，增词不是随意的，而是基于汉英两种语言表达方式的差异，增加一些词，以使译文忠信流畅。

（1）根据句法上的需要

通常，在英语中需要省略的句子成分，在翻译中需要补出，这样才能符合汉语的习惯。

【例1】 Hence the reason why this material have minor shinkage.

14

这正是这种材料有较小收缩的原因。（句子是省略句，在 hence 后省略了 that is，翻译中需要补出。）

（2）根据意义上的需要

① 增加量词和助词　英语没有（或省略）量词、助词（着、了、过、已经）等，汉译时应该根据上下文的需要增补。

【例2】　This building was at last <u>finished</u> with the cooperation of all our staffs.

在全体员工的合作之下，这个建筑终于<u>完工了</u>。

② 增加表示复数和时态的词　汉语名词没有复数的概念，动词没有时态的变化，翻译时有必要增加表示复数和时态的词，有时候甚至要添加表示时间对比的词。

【例3】　Important <u>data</u> have been obtained after a series of experiments.

在一系列的试验之后，得到<u>了许多</u>重要的数据。

【例4】　This materail <u>used to</u> be widely applied to engineering construction. It never <u>has been</u> out of use and never <u>will</u>.

<u>过去</u>，这种材料在建筑施工中被广泛采用。现在它们<u>仍然</u>没有过时，<u>将来也不会</u>。

③ 增加抽象名词　在含有动作意义的抽象名词之后增加"作用"、"现象"、"效用"、"方案"、"过程"、"情况"、"设计"、"变化"等词，以表示具体概念。

【例5】　<u>Oxidation</u> will make iron and steel rusty.

<u>氧化作用</u>会使钢铁生锈。

④ 增加动词　根据意义的需要，可以在名词或动名词前后增加动词。通常增加的汉语动词有："进行"、"出现"、"产生"、"引起"、"发生"、"遭遇"、"使"等。

【例6】　Testing is a complicated problem and long experience is required for its mastery.

<u>进行试验</u>是一个复杂的问题，需要有长期的经验才能掌握。

⑤ 增加解说性词　当英语的某些词单独译出意思不明确时，可在其前增加解说性词使译文意思明确。

【例7】　The compressive strength decreases with the dosage of water.

抗压强度随水量的<u>增加</u>而下降。

⑥ 增加概括性词　在句子中有几个并列成分时，可在其后增添表示数量概念的概括词，达到一定的修辞效果。

【例8】　A student must have a good foundation in chemistry, physics mechanics, dynamics and strength of materials.

设计人员必须在化学、物理、机械和材料力学这<u>四个方面</u>有良好的基础。

（3）根据修辞上的需要

英译汉时，有时需要在译文中增加一些起连贯作用的词，主要是连词、副词和代词，以达到使句子连贯、行文流畅的修辞目的。

【例9】　The Japanese have developed a new type of machine called moles, which can bore through soft and hard rock by mechanical means.

日本人已研制出一种名叫鼹鼠掘进机的新型机械，这种掘进机使用机械方法，<u>既</u>可挖掘软岩<u>又</u>可挖掘硬岩。

【例10】　It is necessary that the calculations should be made accurately.

计算要精确，<u>这一点</u>是很有必要的。

（4）重复原文中出现过的词

英语中常常会有几个名词共用一个动词，几个形容词共用一个中心词，或是为了避免重复用代词替换先行词等现象。翻译时需要重复原文重要的或关键的词，以期达到使译文清楚或是强调的作用。另外，将多宾语、状语或表语的动词采用不同的形式分别译出，以便于行文。

【例 11】 An alternative way to use reinforcement is to stretch <u>it</u> by hydraulic jacks before the concrete is poured around <u>it</u>.

另一种方法是先用液压千斤顶把钢筋拉长，然后在<u>钢筋</u>周围浇灌混凝土。（重复代词所指代的对象）

【例 12】 A synthetic material equal to that alloy in strength has been created, <u>which</u> is very useful in civil engineering.

一种在强度上和那种合金相等的合成材料已经制造出来了，<u>这种合金材料</u>在土木工程中很有用。（重复关系代词所指代的先行词）

【例 13】 A body <u>may be exposed</u> to one constant stress, or to variable stress, of even to compound stress, that is where several stresses act on it at the same time.

一个物体可能<u>经受</u>一个不变的应力，或者<u>经受</u>一个变化的应力，甚至可能<u>经受</u>复合的应力，即同时有几个应力作用在它上面。（重复带多个宾语的动词）

【例 14】 Ice is the solid state, water the liquid state, and water vapor the gaseous state.

冰是固态的，水<u>是</u>液态的，而水蒸气<u>是</u>气态的。（重复句中省略的部分）

【例 15】 Also there has been a concreted effort to modernize and <u>increase</u> space, facilities, equipment, and supporting materials used in science teaching.

而且，大家协同努力，从而<u>扩大</u>了场地，<u>发展</u>了机构，<u>增添</u>了设备和科学教育用的辅助材料，并使之现代化。

2.5.2　Methods of Omitting　省译法

所谓省译就是将原文中的某些词语略去不译。在不损害原文内容的基础上，删去一些不必要的词语，会使行文更加简洁明快，充分体现科技文献的一大特点。总体来说，英译汉时省译的现象比增译的现象相对更多。比如说，冠词属于英语里出现频率较高的词，但在汉语里没有，一般可以不译；而有的词如介词、连接词和代词等，在英语里出现频率较高，但汉语则可以通过借助语序表达逻辑关系，所以这几类词有时可以省略。

（1）省略冠词

【例 16】 <u>The</u> cement is <u>the</u> important part of <u>the</u> concrete.

水泥是混凝土中的重要组成部分。

当然，在英语的一些词组中，冠词的存在使词组的意义发生了很大的变化，所以要另加注意。例如，out of the question（毫无可能，不值得考虑）和 out of question（毫无疑问，不成问题），冠词虽不用特别译出，但是词组的意思刚好相反，这一点在翻译时要体现出来。

（2）省略代词

【例 17】 If you know the internal forces, <u>you</u> can determine the proportion of members.

如果知道内力，就能确定构件尺寸。

（3）省略介词

【例18】 The critical temperature is different <u>for</u> different kinds of steel.

不同类的钢，其临界温度各不相同。

（4）省略动词

【例19】All kinds of excavators <u>perform</u> basically similar function but <u>appear</u> in a variety of forms.

各种挖土机的作用基本相同，但形式不同。

（5）省略连词

【例20】 <u>If</u> there are no heat-treatment, meals can not be made so hard.

没有热处理，金属就不会变得如此坚硬。

【例21】 Up <u>and</u> down motion can be changed to circular motion.

上下运动可以改变为圆周运动。

（6）省略名词

介词 of 前表示度量意义的名词有时可以省略不译。

【例22】 Different <u>kinds</u> of matter have different properties.

不同物质具有不同的特性。

（7）省略意义上重复的词

英语中常用 or 引出同位语，这些同位语有的可分别译出，有的具有相同的译名，只能译出一个，省略一个。有时句子里个别词与其他词意义重复，翻译时也应予以省略。

【例23】The mechanical energy can be changed back into electrical energy by means of a <u>generator or dynamo</u>.

机械能可利用发电机再转变成电能。（省略同位语 dynamo）

2.6　Translation of Special Sentence Pattern 特殊句型的翻译

科技英语中，经常出现被动句型、否定句型、强调句型等。这些句型都有其自身特点，往往和汉语句型有一些不同，在翻译时容易造成错误，因而要特别注意。

2.6.1　Passive Sentence Pattern 被动句型

与汉语相比，英语中被动语态使用的范围要广泛得多。凡是出现以下情况，英语常用被动语态：不必说出行动的行为者；无从说出行动的行为者；不便说出行动的行为者等。英语被动语态的句子，译成汉语时，很多情况下都可译成主动句，但也有一些可以保持被动语态。

（1）译成汉语主动句

① 原文中的主语在译文中仍作主语，将被动语态的谓语译成"加以……"，"是……的"等。

【例1】 Tents are still used by necessity by some nomads or by modern people who want to experience the type of life our ancestors lived.

那些流浪汉或者是想体验我们祖先生活的现代人会用帐篷。

② 原文中的主语在译文中作宾语，将英语句译成汉语的无主语句，或加译"人们"、

"我们"、"大家"、"有人"等词作主语。

【例2】 <u>Attempts are also being made</u> to produce concrete with more strength and durability, and with a lighter weight.

目前仍在尝试生产强度更高、耐久性更好，而且重量更轻的混凝土。（无主语）

③ 用英语句中的动作者（通常放在介词 by 后）作汉语句中的主语。

【例3】 The top layers was bound together more firmly <u>by mixing the crushed rock with asphalt</u>.

用沥青掺拌碎石能使表层更坚固地黏结在一起。

④ 将英语句中的一个适当成分译成汉语句中的主语。

【例4】 Much progress has been made in <u>material science</u> in less than one century.

不到一个世纪，材料学取得了许多进展。

（2）译作汉语被动句

原句中的主语仍译成主语，而原句中的被动意义用"被"，"受到……"，"使……"等词来表达。

【例5】 The model equation is reconciled by mathematical calculation with the actual situation.

通过数学计算使模型方程符合实际情况。

【例6】 Durability is greatly influenced by concrete permeability.

混凝土的耐久性受其渗透性影响非常大。

【例7】 The compressive strength of concrete is controlled by the amount of cement, aggregates, water, and various admixtures contained in the mix.

混凝土的抗压强度为水泥、集料、水及混合料中所含的各种添加剂的用量所控制。

（3）把原句中的被动语态谓语动词分离出来，译成一个独立结构

【例8】 It is believed that the automobile is blamed for such problems as urban area expansion and wasteful land use, congestion and slum conditions in the central areas, and air and noise pollution.

有人认为汽车造成一系列问题，如城市膨胀、土地浪费、市区拥挤、油污遍地以及空气和噪声污染等。

这种方法常用于一些固定句型中，类似的结构还有：

It is asserted that …	有人主张……
It is suggested that …	有人建议……
It is stressed that …	有人强调说……
It is generally considered that …	大家认为……
It is told that …	有人曾经说……
It is well known that …	众所周知……

有时，某些固定句型翻译时不加主语，如：

It is hoped that …	希望……
It is supposed that …	据推测……
It is said that …	据说……

It must be admitted that …   必须承认……

It must be pointed out that …   必须指出……

It will be seen from this that …   由此可见……

2.6.2　Negative Sentence Pattern　否定句型

英语的否定句多种多样。与我们所熟知的一般否定形式不同的是，英语中有一些特殊的否定句，其否定形式与否定概念不是永远一致的，它们所表达的含义、逻辑等都和我们从字面上理解的有很大差别。总之，英语当中的否定问题是一种常见而又复杂的问题，值得特别的重视。

（1）否定成分的转译

否定成分的转译是指由意义上的一般否定转为其他否定（特指否定），反之亦然。常见的句型有：

① "not…so…as…" 结构

在谓语否定的句子中，如果带有 so…as 连接的比较状语从句，或 as 连接的方式状语从句，就应该译成"不像……那样……"，而不能直译成"像……那样不……"；

【例9】　The sun's rays do not warm the water so much as they do the land.

太阳光线使水增温不如它们使陆地增温那样高。

② "not…think/believe…" 结构

表示对某一问题持否定见解的句子，要把英语里面谓语动词 think，believe 等后面的否定词 not 转译到后面，即译为"认为……不……"、"觉得……不是……"；

【例10】　Ordinarily we don't think air as having weight.

我们通常认为空气没有重量。

③ "not…because…" 结构

在汉语时要注意的是，这种结构可以表示两种不同的否定含义，既可以否定谓语，也可以否定原因状语 because，因为汉译时要根据上下文意思来判断。

【例11】　This version is not placed first because it is simple.

这个方案并不因为简单而放在首位。

这个方案因为太简单所以不能放在首位。

以上的两种翻译实际上都是可以的。但是如果在上面的例子后面再加上一句"We need a more particular one which could explain every specific steps we have to take care of." 那么，就只能选择第二种译法了。

（2）否定语气的改变

英语中的否定句并非一概译成汉语的否定句，有些否定句表达的是肯定的意思，常见的是 nothing but 句型；有些在特定的语义环境下也表达肯定意思。

【例12】　Early computer did nothing but compute: adding, subtraction, multiplying and dividing.

早期的计算机只能做加减乘除运算。

（3）部分否定

英语中 all, both, every, each, always 等词与 not 搭配使用时，表示部分否定。一般译成"不是都"、"不总是"、"不全是"。

【例 13】 <u>All</u> these building materials are <u>not</u> good products.

这些建筑材料并不都是优质产品。（不能译成"所有这些建筑材料都不是优质产品"）

类似的结构还有："not…many"（不多），"not…much"（一些），"not…often"（不经常）。应该说明的是，"all…not…"和"not all…"这两种表示部分否定的形式，前者是传统的说法，虽然不合逻辑，但习惯上使用；后者是新说法，从逻辑和语法上着眼，认为比较合理，所以越来越多的人采用的是后一种用法，尤其在美国书刊中更为常见。

（4）意义否定

有些句子当中没有出现否定词，但句中含有表示否定的词或词组，那么汉译时一般要将其否定意义译出，成为汉语的否定句。

【例 14】 The analysis is too complicated us to complete the computation on time.

分析工作太复杂，难以按时完工。

【例 15】 He gained little advantage from the scheme.

他从这项计划中没有得到多少利益。

常见的含有否定意义的词组还有：

but for	如果没有	in the dark	一点也不知道
free from	没有，免于	safe from	免于
short of	缺少	far from	远非，一点也不
in vain	无效，徒劳	but that	要不是，若非
make light of	不把……当一回事	fail to	没有

（5）双重否定

① 针对同一事物的否定　有些词句在形式上是否定，而意思却是双重否定，也就是两个否定，即语法否定（not）和语义否定（非 not 否定词的词或词组否定，如 unexpected），都是针对同一事物而言，是"否定的否定"。

【例 16】 With a careful study of all the preliminary data made available to this engineer, there could be <u>nothing unexpected</u> about the problem.

通过这位工程师对所有初测资料进行审慎研究，这个问题就一切都在意料之中了。

【例 17】 There is no material but will deform more or less under the action of force.

在力的作用下，没有一种材料不或多或少地发生变形。（but 作关系代词，相当于that…not）

常见的搭配还有："not…until"（直到……之后，才能）"not(none)…the less"（并不……就不），"not a little"（大大地）。

② 针对两种不同事物的否定

两个否定分别针对两种不同事物而言，"不是否定的否定"，只是一句话里存在两个否定含义的词汇而已。

【例 18】 There is no steel not containing carbon.

没有不含碳的钢。

【例 19】 One body never exerts a force upon anther without the second reacting against the first.

一个物体对另一个物体施作用力必然会受到反作用力。

2.6.3　Emphatical Sentence Pattern　强调句型

强调句型 "It is (was) + 被强调部分 + that (which, who)..." 几乎可用于强调任何一个陈述句的主语、宾语或状语。需要注意的是，此强调句型与带形式主语 it 的主语从句很相似，但它与主语从句不同的是，去掉以上几个英文单词以后，强调句中剩下的单词仍能组成一个完整的句子。

【例20】　It is these drawbacks which need to be eliminated and which have led to the search for new material.

正因为有这些缺点需要消除，才导致了对新材料的研究探求。

【例21】　It is this kind of steel that the construction worksite needs most urgently.

建筑工地最急需的正是这种钢。

"It is (was) not until + 时间状语 + that..." 是强调时间状语常见的一种句型，可译成"直到……才……"。

【例22】　It is not until 1936 that a great new bridge was built across the Forth at Kincardine.

直到1936年才在肯卡丁建成一座横跨海口的新大桥。

在强调句中，被强调的部分不仅可以是一个词或词组，而且还可以是一个状语从句。

【例23】　It is not until the stiff concrete can be placed and vibrated properly to obtain the designed strength in the field that the high permissible compressive stress in concrete can be utilized.

只有做到在工地正确灌注振捣干硬性混凝土并使之达到设计强度时，才能充分利用混凝土容许压应力。

2.7　Translation of Long Sentence　长句的翻译

长句一般都是含有几个错综复杂关系的主从复句或并列复句，少数则是难用汉语表达的简单句。英语长句的理解，关键在于语法分析。具体来说，理解长句大体可以分为两个步骤进行：

① 判断出句子是简单句、并列句，还是主从句；

② 先找出句中的主要成分，即主语和谓语动词，然后再分清句中的宾语、状语、表语、宾语补足语、定语等。

英语长句的翻译主要采用分句和改变语序的方法，具体包括顺译法、倒译法和拆译法等。

2.7.1　Methods of Translation in Order Sentence　顺译法

对专业英语而言，只要不太违反汉语的行文习惯和表达方式，一般应尽量采用顺译。顺译有两个长处：一是可以基本保留英语语序，避免漏译，力求在内容和形式两方面贴近原文；二是可以顺应长短句相替、单复句相间的汉语句法修辞原则。

（1）在主谓连接处切断

【例1】　The main problem in the design of the foundations of a multi-storey building under while the soil settles is to keep the total settlement of the building within reasonable limits, but specially to see that the relative settlement from one column to the next is not great.

在土壤沉降处设计多层建筑基础的主要问题，就是要使建筑物的总沉降量保持在合理的限度内，而且特别要注意相邻柱子之间的相对沉降量不能过大。

（2）在并列或转折连接处切断

【例2】 The Portland cement and concrete industries have already done great efforts to become greener industries,but more can be done.

尽管水泥与混凝土企业已经付出了很大的努力来使企业更环保,但在这方面企业还需要付出更多。

【例3】 One of the main drawbacks of lime as a binder is that it loses part of its strength when it comes into contact with water due to partial dissolution of calcium carbonate

石灰作为作为胶凝材料的缺点之一就是，当它遇到水之后会强度会降低，这是因为氢氧化钙中水中溶解了的缘故。

（3）在从句前切断

【例4】 As concrete's advantages outweigh its weaknesses, it is not surprising that concrete is presently the most widely used material after water.

随着混凝土的优点胜过其缺憾点,混凝土作为水之后又一被广泛应用的材料就不足为怪了。

2.7.2 Methods of Translation in Inverted Sentence 倒译法

在英译汉时,常常需根据汉语的行文习惯表达方式将英语长句进行全部倒置或局部倒置。当然,翻译时不一定非倒译,在大多数情况下,倒置也只是一种变通手段,并不是唯一可行的办法。

（1）将英语原句全部倒置

【例5】 The first tall structure using steel as its principal building material was the Eiffel Tower in Paris.

法国的埃菲尔铁塔是第一个将钢材作为主要建筑材料的建筑物。

（2）将英语原句部分倒置（将句首或首句置于全句之尾）

2.7.3 Methods of Translation in Taking Apart 拆译法

为汉语行文方便,有时将英文原文的某一短语或从句先行单独译出,并利用适当的概括性词语或通过一定的语法手段把它同主语联系在一起,进行重新组织。

【例6】 An innovative building approach that incorporates high standards of environmental protection,often uses high performance materials.

对环境保护要求比较高的创新性的建筑方法，往往使用了高性能的建筑材料。

【例7】 The integrated products quality control system used by thousands of enterprises in Russia is a combination of controlling bodies and objects under control interacting with the help of material, technical and information facilities when exercising QC at the level of an enterprise.

俄罗斯成千上万家企业采用的产品质量综合管理体系,是通过在整个企业范围内实行质量管理、把企业内各个管理机构和各种管理对象联结一起的综合体,这种联结是借助于材料部门、技术部门和信息部门实现的。

2.8 Translation of Subordinate Clause 从句的翻译

英语句子的某些成分由句子代替了单词以后，就形成了主从复合句。英语的主从复合句按语法功能来分有主语从句、宾语从句、定语从句、状语从句、表语从句和同谓语从句。主从复合句由于其结构比简单句复杂，并且从句相对扩充以后能使复合句的结构更加复杂，因而它往往也是英语翻译时一个必须重视的问题。

2.8.1 主语从句和宾语从句 （Subject Clause and Object Clause）

在专业英语中，较常使用带形式主语 it 的主语从句，即句子常用引导词 it 作形式主语并放在句首，而把从句（真正的主语）放在谓语之后。

（1）译成宾语从句

【例 1】 It is generally accepted that fatigue strength is drastically lower if the concrete is cracked.

人们普遍认为，混凝土若出现裂缝，其疲劳强度就会大大降低。

（2）译成并列分句

【例 2】 It remains to be confirmed that epoxy coatings will retain their integrity over long periods of time in alkaline environments.

长期处于碱性环境中的环氧涂层能否保持其完好无损的性能，这有待进一步研究证实。

（3）谓语分译

【例 3】 It is a fact that no structural material is perfectly elastic.

事实上，没有一种结构是完全的弹性体。

（4）宾语从句

常见的形式宾语句的真实宾语也有三种：从句、不定式或动名词。形式宾语 it 和后面的说明语（多为形容词）在逻辑上是主表关系。它的翻译方法和形式主语句类同。

2.8.2 Attributive Clause 定语从句

定语从句在英语中的应用极广。由于英语中定语从句有长有短，结构有简有繁，对先行词的限制有强有弱，翻译时就不能一概对待，必须根据每个句子的特点，结合上下文灵活处理。一般来说，定语从句在逻辑意义上往往与所限定的词有着表示"目的"、"结果"、"原因"、"让步"等含义。因此，在英译汉时，需要先弄清定语从句与先行词的逻辑关系。

（1）译成前置定语

限制性定语从句往往译成前置定语结构，即译成"……的"。但有些非限定性定语从句有时也可以作前置处理，尤其是当从句本身较短，或与被修饰词关系较为密切，或因拆译造成译文结构松散时。

【例 4】 A drainage blanket is a layer of material that has a very high coefficient of permeability.

排水层为渗透系数较大的材料层。

【例 5】 In the design of concrete structures, an engineer can specify the type of material that he will use.

在混凝土结构设计中，工程师可以指定他将要使用的材料品种。

（2）译成谓语

当关系代词在定语从句中充当主语且句子的重点是在从句上时，可省去关系代词，而将定语从句的其余部分译为谓语结构，以先行词充当它的主语，从而使先行词与定语从句合译成一句。

【例6】 A code is a set of specifications and standards <u>that control important technical specifications of design and construction</u>.

一套规范和标准可以<u>控制设计和施工的许多重要技术细节</u>。

（3）译成并列句

非限制性定语从句往往需要拆译成并列句，有时，限制性定语从句因从句本身太长，前置会使句子显得臃肿，故也可采用拆译分列。

【例7】 The tendons are frequently passed through continuous channels formed by metal or plastic ducts, <u>which</u> are positioned securely in the forms before the concrete is cast.

预应力钢筋束穿入用金属管或塑料管制成的连续孔道,<u>而金属管或塑料管</u>在浇筑混凝土之前被固定在模板之中。

（4）译成状语从句

定语从句有时与主语之间的关系，实际上是原因、条件、目的、让步、结果、转折等隐含逻辑关系。因此，英译汉时应以逻辑为基础，以忠实表达原文的意思为前提，将定语从句转译成汉语的状语从句。

【例8】 This is particularly important in fine-grained soils <u>where</u> the water can be sucked up near the surface by capillary attraction.

在细颗粒土壤中这一点尤其重要，<u>因为</u>在这种土壤中，由于毛细作用，水能被吸引到靠近道路表面的地方。（译成原因状语从句）

（5）译成单句中的一部分

限制性定语从句有时在翻译时可压缩成宾语、谓语、表语和同位语。

【例9】 Fig. 1 incorporates many of the factors <u>which must be considered</u> in analysing a new material.

图1所示的许多因素，在分析一种新材料时<u>必须予以考虑</u>。

2.8.3 Adverbial Clause 状语从句

状语从句相对而言比较简单,但有几点关于时间状语从句和地点状语从句的情况值得注意。

（1）时间状语从句

时间状语从句在英语句中的位置相对灵活，但汉译时，有时候就要注意它们的位置问题。汉语习惯是先发生的事情先讲，表示时间的从句汉译时要提前。当时间顺序很明显时，有时还可以省略关系副词。

【例10】 Pre-tensioning is a method of prestressing in which the steel tendons are tensioned before the concrete has been placed in the moulds.

先张法是一种在往模板内浇筑混凝土之前，即将钢筋束张拉而施加预应力的方法。

值得注意的是，有时看似由 when, while 等引导的时间状语从句，实际上却是具有条件状语从句或是让步状语从句的意义，即相当于 if, although 引导的状语从句，翻译时往往可以转译成条件状语从句。

【例11】 On the site when further information becomes available, the engineer can make changes in his sections and layout, but the drawing office work will not have been lost.

在现场若能取得更确切的资料，工程师就可以修改他所做的断面图和设计图，但是绘图室的工作并非徒劳无功。

（2）地点状语从句

由 where 引导的状语从句，有时不宜译作地点状语从句，因为原文实际上所表达的不是地点意义而是条件意义，状语从句起着条件状语的作用。因此，若遇到这类地点状语从句时，一般可以转译成条件状语从句。

【例12】 Where internal corrosion is known to exist, the following practices can be employed.

如果发现有内腐蚀的存在，可采用以下措施。

2.9 Translation about Quantity 有关数量的翻译

2.9.1 Doubled and Redoubled Addition 成倍增加

（1）表示数量成倍增加的句型

基本句型有以下几种：

A is N times are large (long, heavy, …) as B.

A is N times larger (longer, heavier, …) than B.

A is larger (longer, heavier, …) than B by N times.

上述几个句型的含义相同，均可译成：A 的大小（长度、质量……）是 B 的 N 倍，或 A 比 B 大（长、重……）N−1 倍。

【例1】 The temperature on the site may be to 40 times higher in summer as compared to winter.

工地的夏季气温可能是冬季气温的 40 倍。

（2）表示倍数的单词

有些单词可直接表示倍数关系，如 double（增加一倍，翻一番），treble（增加两倍，或增加到三倍），quadruple（增加三倍，翻两番）等。

【例2】 If the speed is doubled, keeping the radius constant, the centripetal force becomes four times as great.

若保持半径不变，速度增大一倍，则向心力增大为原来的 4 倍。（即增大了 3 倍）

还有些表示增加的动词（如 increase）加上 N times, by N times, N-fold 等来表达"增加 N 倍"的含义。

【例3】 Such construction procedure can increase productivity over threefold.

这种施工工序可使生产率提高到 3 倍以上。（即提高了 2 倍多）

2.9.2 Doubled and Redoubled Redcution 成倍减少

语句中表示成倍减少含义时，通常包含以下句子成分：

reduce by N times

reduce N times

reduce to N times

reduce N times as much (many…) as

reduce by a factor of N

reduce N-fold

N-fold reduction	N times less than

对上述结构，均可译成"减少了（N−1）/N"或"减少到原来的 1/N"。

【例 4】 The production cost has reduced four times.

生产成本减少了 3/4。（即减少到原来的 1/4）

【例 5】 The advantage of the present scheme lies in a fivefold reduction in manpower.

这一方案的优点在于节约人工 4/5。（即节约到原来的 1/5）

2.9.3　Uncertain Quantity　不确定数量

英语中常用来修饰不确定数量的词有：circa, about, around, some, nearly, roughly, approximately, or so, more or less, in the vicinity of, in the neighborhood of, a matter of, of the order of 等。这些词可译成"大约……"、"接近……"、"……上下"、"……左右"等。

【例 6】　a weight around 12 tons　　　　12 吨左右的重量

　　　　　300km or so　　　　　　　　大约 300 公里

　　　　　a force of the order of 100KN　约为 100 千牛的力

另外，还有一些表示不确定数量量级的词组，如：

teens of…	十几（13～19）	tens of…	几十
decades of…	几十	dozens of…	几打
scores of…	几十（多于 40）	hundreds of…	几百
thousands of…	几千		

另外，度量单位的英语表达及换算可参见 Appendix。

Exercises

Translate the following into Chinese.

1. Rock made under water tell another story.

2. Force is any push or pull that tends to produce or prevent motion.

3. A prediction of the duration of the period when building materials cannot be supplied would be of value in the planning of construction.

4. Our present-day civilization could never have evolved without the skills included in the field of engineering.

5. In a large structure expansion joints are always provided so that the material may be allowed to expand.

6. Bituminous seals are placed on the joints between concrete slabs to prevent the ingress of water.

7. This paper aims at discussing the properties of the newly discovered material.

8. The combination of mechanical properties of this alloy can be well achieved by heat treatment.

9. The Congressman tends to be very interested in public works — such as a new government buildings, water projects, highways and bridges, etc. — that will bring money to the area or improve living conditions.

10. For any unusual structure the tasks of design and analysis will have to be repeated many times until, after many calculations, a design has been found that is strong, stable and lasting.

Unit 3　Writing of Scientific and Technical Papers

撰写英文科技论文的目的，是为了参与国际间学术交流，如在英文期刊杂志上发表或在国际学术会议上宣读自己的科技论文，让同行了解和分享你的学术成果。

为提高论文写作质量、减少撰写过程中的盲目性，有必要较系统地了解和学习英文科技论文的写作方法。本章结合土木工程，介绍英文科技论文写作的一般方法；并通过实例，解释写作要点和技巧。

3.1　Stylistic Rules of Papers　论文体例

国际标准化组织（International Organization for Standardization）、美国国家标准化协会（American National Standards Institute）和英国标准协会（British Standards Institute）等国际组织都对期刊类科技论文的写作体例（stylistic rules）做出了规定，其基本内容如下。

3.1.1　Composition about Papers in Periodical　期刊类论文组成

- Title 标题
- Abstract 摘要
- Keywords 关键词，或主题词(Subjects)
- Main text 正文
  Introduction 引言
  Analysis of the theory, test procedure 理论分析或试验过程
  Results 结果
  Discussions (Summary, Conclusions, Suggestion and Development) 讨论（总结，结论，建议和发展）
- Acknowledgments 致谢（可以没有）
- References (Appendix) 参考文献（附录）

3.1.2　Science Report　长篇科技报告

长篇科学报告包括科研成果、学位论文、可行性研究等。

（1）FRONT 文前
- Front cover 封面
  Title 标题
  Contract or job number 合同或任务号
  Author or authors 作者
  Date of issue 完成日期
  Report number and serial number 报告编写和系列编号
  Name of organization responsible for the report 研究单位名称
  A classification notice 密级
- Title page 扉页

- Letter of transmittal (Forwarding letter) 提交报告书
- Distribution list 分发范围
- Preface or foreword 序或前言
- Acknowledgments 致谢（可以没有）
- Abstract 摘要
- Table of contents 目录
- List of illustration 图表目录

（2）MAIN TEXT 正文
- Introduction 引言
- Analysis of the theory, test procedure 理论分析或试验过程
- Results 结果
- Discussions (Summary, Conclusions, Suggestion and Development) 讨论（总结，结论，建议和发展）

（3）BACK 文后
- References 参考文献
- Appendix 附录
- Tables 表
- Graphics 图
- List of abbreviations, signs and symbols 缩写、记号和符号表
- Index 索引
- Back cover 封底

实际写作中，不一定也不可能完全按上述内容编写，视具体情况和要求确定。

3.2　Title and Sign 标题与署名

论文标题属于特殊文体，一般不采用句子，而是采用名词、名词词组或名词短语的形式，通常省略冠词。从内容上，要求论文标题能突出地、明确地反映出论文主题。具体而言，在拟定论文标题时应注意以下几点：

① 恰如其分而又不过于笼统地表现论文的主题和内涵；

② 单词的选择要规范化，要便于二次文献编制题录、索引、关键词等；

③ 尽量使用名词性短语，字数控制在两行之内。

【例1】　Bayesian Technique for Evaluation of Material Strengths in Existing Structures 采用贝叶斯技术评估既有结构的材料强度

3.2.1　Normal Format of Writing Title 标题书写的几种常用格式

（1）标题主要单词首字母大写，其余小写

【例2】　Bridge Live-Load Models

（2）标题主要单词首字母大写，其余为小型大写

【例3】　NONLINEAR ANALYSIS OF SPACE TRUSSES

（3）标题文字全部大写

【例4】　RELIABILITY ASSESSMENT OF PRESTRESSED CONCRETE BEAMS

（4）标题首单词首字母大写

【例5】 Sustainable development slowed down by bad construction practices and natural and technological disasters

3.2.2 Sign and Information of Author 署名和有关作者信息

一般，紧跟在论文标题之后的是论文署名和有关作者的信息，如作者单位、通信地址（近年来还包括 E-mail 地址，个人主页的网址）、职称、学衔或会员情况等。按照英语国家的习惯，论文署名时名在前（可缩写），姓在后；但为了便于计算机检索，也有姓在前、名在后的情况（参考文献中的作者姓名的排列就是这样）。有关作者的信息有时放在署名之后，有时放在论文第一页的页脚，有时放在论文的末尾，有时还分开编排，这要视论文载体的具体要求而定。

【例6】 作者信息紧接在署名之后。

Developing Expert Systems for Structural Diagnostics and Reliability

Assessment at J.R.C

A.C.Lucia

Commission of the European Communities, Joint Research Center,

ISPRA Establishment, 21020 ISPRA (VA), Italy

【例7】 作者信息放在论文第一页的页脚。

BRIDGE RELIABILITY EVALUATION USING LOAD TESTS

By AndrzejS.Nowak[1] and T.Tharmabala[2]

在论文第一页的页脚：

[1]Assoc.prof.of Civ. Engrg.,Univ.of Michigan,Ann Arbor,MI 48109

[2]Res.Ofcr.,Ministry of Transp. and Communications, Downvsview, Ontario,Canada M3M 1J8

注意，在作者信息以及参考文献内，为节省篇幅，会采用较多的甚至不常见的缩写。

如下例中的 Assoc 为 Associate, Civ 为 Civil, Engrg 为 Engineering, MI 为 Michigan, Res 为 Research, Ofcr 为 Officer, Transp 为 Transportation 等。

3.3 Abstract 摘要

摘要（Abstract）是一篇科技论文的核心体现，直接影响读者对论文的第一印象。一篇学术价值较高的论文，若摘要撰写得不理想，会使论文价值大打折扣。因此，掌握英文摘要的特点是非常重要的。

3.3.1 The Basic Characters of Abstract 摘要的基本特点

① 能使读者理解全文的基本要素，能脱离原文而独立存在。

② 摘要是对原文的精华提炼和高度概括，信息量大。

③ 具有客观性和准确性。

3.3.2 The Form and Requirement of Contents 形式和内容要求

摘要和基本形式和内容表现在以下几方面。

① 若无特殊的规定，一般摘要位于论文标题和正文之间，但有时也要求接在正文之后。

② 对于一般篇幅的论文，摘要的篇幅控制在 80～100 个单词左右；对于长篇报告或学位论文，摘要的篇幅控制在 250 个单词左右，一般不超过 500 个单词。

③ 一般篇幅论文摘要不分段，长篇报告或学位论文的摘要可分段，但段落不宜太多。

④ 与标题写作相反，摘要需采用完整的句子，不能使用短语；另外，要注意使用一些转折词连接前后语句，避免行文过于干涩单调。

⑤ 避免使用大多数人暂时还不熟悉或容易引起误解的单词缩写和符号等；不可避免时，应对这些单词缩写和符号在摘要中第一次出现处加以说明；例如：TM（Technical Manual）、CCES(Chinese Civil Engineering Society)等。

⑥ 摘要的句型少用或不用第一人称，多采用第三人称被动语态，以体现客观性。

⑦ 避免隐晦和模糊，采用准确、简洁的语句概括全文所描述的目的、意义、观点、方法和结论等。

⑧ 注意体现摘要的独立性和完整性，使读者在不参看原文的情况下就能基本了解论文的内容；摘要的观点和结论必须与原文一致，忌讳把原文没有的内容写入摘要。

⑨ 通常摘要采用一个主题句（Topic sentence）开头，以阐明论文的主旨，或引出论文的研究对象，或铺垫论文的工作等，避免主题句与论文标题的完全或基本重复。

⑩ 摘要之后，通常要附上若干个表示全文内容的关键词或主题词或检索词（Indexing term），应选用规范化的、普遍认可的单词、词组或术语作为关键词，不宜随心编造。

3.3.3　The Sentences Pattern in Common Use　常用句型

在撰写摘要时，可套用一些固定句型。不过，掌握句型和词汇特点，并结合实际情况灵活运用，更为重要。下列几个句型仅供参考 。

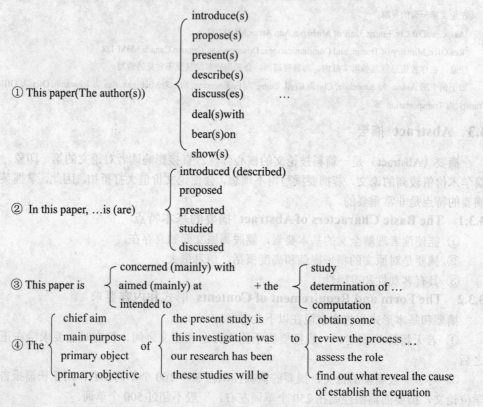

30

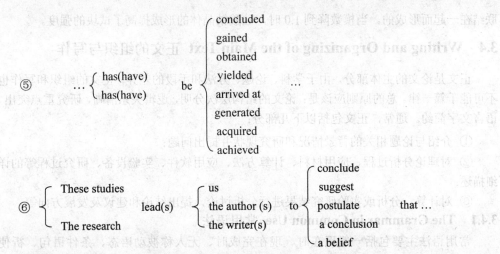

⑤ ... $\left\{\begin{array}{l}\text{has(have)}\\\text{has(have)}\end{array}\right\}$ be $\left\{\begin{array}{l}\text{concluded}\\\text{gained}\\\text{obtained}\\\text{yielded}\\\text{arrived at}\\\text{generated}\\\text{acquired}\\\text{achieved}\end{array}\right\}$ ...

⑥ $\left\{\begin{array}{l}\text{These studies}\\\text{The research}\end{array}\right\}$ lead(s) $\left\{\begin{array}{l}\text{us}\\\text{the author (s)}\\\text{the writer(s)}\end{array}\right\}$ to $\left\{\begin{array}{l}\text{conclude}\\\text{suggest}\\\text{postulate}\\\text{a conclusion}\\\text{a belief}\end{array}\right\}$ that ...

【例1】 This paper presents some recent research on the microstructural development during alkaline activation of slag pastes.

本文介绍了关于研究碱激发矿渣微观结构变化的最新实验。

【例2】 The main purpose of this paper is to present high performance construct material.

本文的主旨是介绍高性能的建筑材料。

【例3】 The book is aimed at telling students how to analyse the microstructure of material.

这本书的目的是教学生们如何分析材料的微观结构。

【例4】 Results of plenty of experiments indicate that the strength decreased when the lime comes into contact with water.

大量的实验结果表明：当石灰遇到水之后强度会降低。

【例5】 The proposed approach may be used as a basic for the analysis of distortion-induced stresses in the concrete box girders.

建议的方法可作为分析混凝土箱梁畸变应力的基础。

3.3.4 The Example of Abstract 摘要实例

这是一篇研究碱激发粉煤灰的文章摘要，标题是：Hardening Mechanisms of an Alkaline-activated Fly Ash（碱激发粉煤灰的硬化机理）。

Abstract: The hardening mechanism of a paste composed of a low calcium fly ash and alkali was investigated. It was found that a fraction of fly ash reacted with water-glass and formed amorph- ous or low-ordered crystalline compounds of the type of $Na_2O-Al_2O_3-SiO_2$, after the paste was cured at 60℃ for 24h. For the water-glass with a modulus of 1.64, the strength of the paste is mainly attributed to the gel-like reaction products that bind the particles of fly ash together. When the modulus is decreased to 1.0, crystalline sodium silicate is formed in the matrix, which helps to achieve high strengths.

摘要：本文研究了低钙粉煤灰与碱组成的胶凝材料的硬化机理，研究发现粉煤灰在水玻璃的作用下在 60℃下养护 24h 后生成了无定形的或者说是低结晶度的 $Na_2O-Al_2O_3-SiO_2$ 型化合物。当水玻璃的模数为 1.64 时，试块强度主要是由于凝胶状的水化产物将粉煤灰联结在一起而形成的。当模数降到 1.0 时，硅酸钠晶体的形成提高了试块的强度。

3.4 Writing and Organizing of the Main Text 正文的组织与写作

正文是论文的主体部分。由于学科、论题、方法和手段的差异，正文的组织和写作也不可能千篇一律。总的原则应该是：论文的结构层次分明，逻辑关系清晰，研究重点突出，语言文字简约。通常，正文包括以下几部分：

① 介绍与论题相关的背景情况和研究现状并提出问题；

② 对理论分析过程、应用材料、计算方法、应用软件、实验设备、研究过程等的详细描述；

③ 对计算、分析或实验研究结果进行分析讨论，提出结论和建议及发展方向等。

3.4.1 The Grammar in Common Use 常用语法

常用语法主要包括一般现在时、现在完成时、无人称被动语态、条件语句、祈使语句等。

（1）一般现在时和现在完成时

在科技类英语的写作中，一般现在时（包括被动语态）用得最多，它常用来描述不受时间限制的客观事实和真理，表达主语的能力、性质、状态和特征等。用得较多的还有现在完成时，但主要是被动语态。它主要用来表述过去发生的（无确切时间），或在过去发生而延续到现在的事件对目前情况的影响。常与现在完成时连用的词有：already、(not) yet、for、since、just、recently、lately 等。

【例 1】 From a structural point of view, a tent <u>is</u> a remarkable structure.

【例 2】 There <u>have been</u> extensive efforts to convert fly ash into useful binding materials by means of alkaline activation.

另外，在论文的引言部分论述某一研究课题的过去情况和目前进展时，时常会用到其他时态，如过去时、现在进行时等。

（2）无人称被动语态

对无需说明或难以说明动作发出者的情况，可用无人称被动语态。

【例 3】 This <u>is shown</u> in fig.1.

【例 4】 Material properties, dimensions, and accuracy of the analytical model <u>are treated</u> as random variables.

（3）条件语句

在理论描述中，常常用到一些条件语句，说明一种假设情况。最常用的条件语句为 if 语句。此外还有其他一些条件表达方式，如：unless (=if…not)、providing (that)、provided (that)、only if、given+名词、in case 、so(as) long as 、suppose (that)、 assume (that)、with…等。

【例 5】 If the time scale is changed to a geological time frame, most of the present concretes will one day end up as a mixture of limestone, clay and gypsum, which are the stable forms of the different mineral oxides used to make it.

【例 6】 <u>Given</u> wind speed and environmental conditions, it is possible to predict the actions by wind on buildings.

【例7】 <u>Provided that</u> the load conditions are known ,the forces on structural members can be analyzed easily.

【例8】 <u>With</u> the equipment the experiment would be readily conducted.

【例9】 L will represent alone the length of the beam in the paper <u>unless otherwise stated</u>.

【例10】 These equations will hold <u>as long as</u> $x<0$.

（4）祈使语句

在理论解释、公式说明和试验分析中，经常会用到祈使语句。它表示指示、说明、建议，或表示条件、假设、设想等。

【例11】 <u>Note that</u> concrete is a porous material and the carbon dioxide from the air can penetrate into the interior of it.

【例12】 <u>Let</u> a equal b in the Equation(1).

【例13】 <u>Be sure to</u> fix the mould board in right position.

【例14】 <u>Suppose that</u> the influence of temperature is negligible the equation cam be rewritten as follows.

3.4.2　The Sentence Pattern in Common Use 常用句型

一般在科技论文撰写中采用符合语法的何种句型，并无一定之规。大量采用的仍是"主+谓+宾"和"主+系+表"结构及复合句型等。不过，有些句型简单明了、适应性广使用频率较高。现列举几种句型如下。

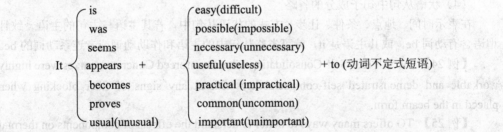

① It ⎰ 系动词+形容词 ⎱ + that 从句
　　 ⎱ 动词 ⎰

② It ＋ 系动词 ＋ 形容词 ＋ to

主要形式有：

It ⎰ is / was / seems / appears / becomes / proves / usual(unusual) ⎱ + ⎰ easy(difficult) / possible(impossible) / necessary(unnecessary) / useful(useless) / practical (impractical) / common(uncommon) / important(unimportant) ⎱ + to (动词不定式短语)

③ 主语+系动词+to（动词不定式短语）

【例15】 <u>It is</u> easy <u>to</u> write a very simple chemical reaction to describe the hydration of calcium sulphate hemihydrate.

【例16】 <u>It is</u> impossible <u>to</u> obtain such a simple spatial organization when Al^{3+} and Mg^{2+} ions are replaced by a larger Ca^{2+} ion.

【例17】 The only problem for the cement producer <u>is to</u> be sure that the grinding mill is fed with a calcium sulphate cocktail that always has the same composition..

3.4.3　The Forms of Omitting 省略形式

专业英语中省略的情况较多，下面只列举几种较常见形式。

（1）用分词独立结构代替从句

当用主句和从句的主语相同时，从句的主语可以省略，用分词独立结构代替从句。句型为：从属连词（before, after, when, while, on, by, in 等）+分词，主语……

【例18】 Before trying to interpret such a curve directly it is best to look at the evolution of the heat rate of C_3S and C_3A pastes.

【例19】 However, when dealing with concretes having a lower water/cement ratio, the very slow solubility rate of natural anhydrite creates problems because as high performance concretes contain a high amount of cement.

（2）用过去分词作后置定语代替定语从句

英语中常用 which、where、what、that 等引导后置定语从句，修饰前面的名词。当后置定语从句中的动词为被动时态时，可省略引导部分，直接用过去分词作后置定语，使句子更简练。下面几个例句括号者中为省略部分。

【例20】 Hydration (which is)being an exothermic reaction, Portland cement hydration is an autoactivated reaction until the temperature stabilizes when thermal losses at the boundaries are equal to the heat liberated by hydration.

【例21】The usual tools (which is) used to define the crystallographic network of minerals were inoperative in the case of C-S-H.

（3）并列复合句的名词成分的省略

在并列复合句中，其第二分句（或后续分句）里常省略与第一分句相同的句子成分（主语、谓语、宾语或状语），见下两例的括号内部分。

【例22】 The bending moment is positive if the beam bends downwards, (the bending moment) negative if (the beam bends)upwards.

【例23】 In Fig.2, R is the resistance, S (is) load effect and K (is) the safety factor.

（4）状语从句中句子成分的省略

在表示时间、地点、条件、让步、方式的状语从句中，若其主语与主句的主语一致且谓语含有动词 be，或其主语是 it，就可省略从句中的主语和作助动词或者连系动词的 be。

【例24】The SCFRC（Self-Consolidating Fiber Reinforced Concrete）mixes were highly workable and demonstrated self-compactability without any signs of fiber blocking when placed in the beam form.

【例25】 TG offers many ways to better understand the effects of components on thermal stability, particularly when combined with infrared spectroscopy.

3.4.4 The Example Sentence and Explanation About Writing 写作例句与说明

写作情况多种多样，可采用的句型也不少。本节根据具体写作对象的不同，介绍一些语句结构、短语和词汇供参考。读者应结合实际情况适当选择并灵活运用，切忌死套。

（1）Progress and Commentary 进展与评述

在科技论文中，尤其在引言部分，往往首先需要对目前进展和他人工作进行评述。对这种情况，通常采用现在完成时态。若干语句结构如下。

① A substantial review of... has been given by...

② An extensive list of references can be found in the review paper by ...

③ …have attracted researchers' attention since…

④ There has been theoretical interest in the field of … for the last decade.

⑤ …have been a major concern in the development of…

⑥ Recently this topic has seen tremendous growth in the theory and methods of..

⑦ Much progress has been made in…

⑧ The last decade has seen tremendous growth in the theory and methods of…

⑨ However, attention was just focused on…,not on…

⑩ Since…have been described in detail elsewhere, only a brief outline of the   important aspects of …is presented here.

⑪…is far from simple and it is therefore desirable to…

⑫ There is a growing need for…

⑬ The problems of…are issues which have increasing important in 1990's

⑭ Some attempts have been made to apply…to…

⑮ It has been shown by…that…have a significant effect on…

⑯ However, it has been observed that…

【例26】 Number of tests has been used to evaluate the performance of coated concrete and these test methods are reviewed with test results reported in the literature.

【例27】 This book is intended to provide some recent progresses and applications of several most commonly used high performance construction materials.

【例28】 A commonly observed problem in these beams is the appearance of end zone cracking due to the prestress forces, hydration of concrete, shrinkage and temperature variation.

（2）Definition and Description 定义与描述

在理论分析和公式推导中，常需要对一个事物或概念做出定义，并进行解释和描述。常见语句结构有：

① Define…to be…

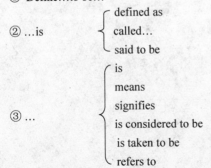

② …is
- defined as
- called…
- said to be

③ …
- is
- means
- signifies
- is considered to be
- is taken to be
- refers to

【例29】 Modulus of elasticity is defined as the ratio of normal stress to corresponding strain for tensile or compressive stresses below the proportional limit of a material.

【例30】 When a powdered admixture is added to factory-made cement during its production, it is called an "additive"and not an admixture.

（3）Hypothesis and Assumption 假说与假设

假说（hypothesis）是在事实基础上根据类比推理、归纳推理和演绎推理提出的。假设（assumption）可用来预测事物发展趋势，简化分析和计算过程。常见语句结构如下。

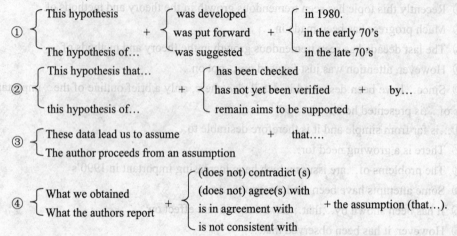

【例31】 According to the theoryadvanced by Litvan, 13 the rigidly held water by the C-S-H (both interlayer and adsorbed in gel pores) in cement paste cannot rearrange itself to form ice at the normal freezing point of water because the mobility of water existing in an ordered state is rather limited.

【例32】What we obtained in the test is in good agreement with the theoretical assumption.

（4）Classification and Comparison 分类与比较

分类与比较是根据事物的特点、属性进行归纳区别，并对两种以上同类事物的异同点或优缺点进行对比，以加深对事物本质的认识。分类语句结构如下。

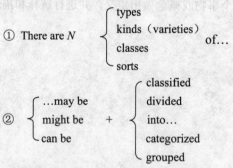

③ There are….,the first …,the second…,…

④ …differs (is different)from…

比较语句结构如下。

⑤ as +adj./adv 原形 +as …和 not so (as)+adj./adv 原形+as…

⑥ 倍数+as…as…

⑦ adj./adv 比较级+than…

36

⑧ …
- (be) superior to
- (be) in advance of
- (have) superiority over …(比……好，优于……)
- (have) advantages over

⑨ …
- (be) inferior to
- (be) nothing to…(比……差，不如)

⑩ …
- bear comparison to(with)
- stand comparison to
- (be) equal to
- (be) comparable to
… (比得上，与……相比)

⑪ 常用短语
- With respect to
- as against
- in comparison to
- as compared to
- compared to (with)
- by the side of
- in contract to
相对于；与……相比；对比起来

【例 33】 The CAC-based expansive additive is generally a dry mixture comprising different types of particulates including calcium alumina cement, calcium sulfate hemihydrate or gypsum, and lime or hydrated lime.

【例 34】 Three types of fasteners will be discussed.

（5）Methods and Means 方法及方式

在阐述研究过程时，总要论及所采用的方法。在专业英语中，对方法的描述往往是句子的状语成分，内容涉及描述方法的类型、途径、意义、范围、方式等。

① by means of
by
with(by)the aid of
by virtue of
in terms of
by the use of
using
使用，采用（某方法）

② mathematically
theoretically
statistically
empirically
experimentally
用数学方法
通过理论探讨，理论上
用统计方法
用经验方法
用实验方法

③ one way or another
in a similar way
in all manner of ways
by some means or other
以某种方法（式）
以类似方法
以各种方法
以某种方法

37

in much the same way	以基本相同的方法			
in a regular manner	以常用方法			
in the usual manner	以常用方法			

④

in a sense	在某种意义上
in all sense, in every sense	在各种意义上
in the same sense	在同样意义上
in this sense	在这个意义上
in a narrow sense	狭义上
in a broad sense	广义上

⑤ 各种方式

without break(intermission)	不间断地
intermittently,with intermittence	间断地
on and on ,continuously	持续不断地
in fits and starts,on and off	断续地
in combination(conjunction)with	与……结合
in isolation	孤立地
independently	独立地
in a discrete fashion	以离散的方式
in an analogous manner	以类似的方式
after the manner(pattern, fashion)of	仿效，仿照
in chronological order	按时间顺序
in descending(ascending)order	以递降（升）顺序
clockwise,in a clockwise sense	顺时针地
counterclockwise	逆时针地

in groups	成群地	upside down	上端朝下
in a line	成直线地	downside up	下端朝上
in pairs	成对地	inside out	里在朝外
in rows	成排地	outside in	外面朝里
in a circle	成圆圈地	the right side up	正面朝上

【例35】 The fibre/matrix composite can have the properties of anisotropy or isotropy by virtue of the arrangement and direction of the fibres in the matrix.

【例36】 Normal range water reducers, e.g., hydrocarboxylic acids, function in a manner similar to their role in portland cement concrete.

（6）Degree and Magnanimity 程度与度量

在论文写作中，需要对事物某一方面的水平进行修辞，以具体或不具体的方式进行度量。这部分内容通常作为句子的定语、表语或状语成分。可参考的词汇或词组如下。

① 显著的；用作定语和表语

pronounced, appreciable, noticeable, conspicuous, considerable, remarkable, marked, significant, substantial 等。

② 显著地，远……得多；作状语

significantly, substantially, considerably, a great deal, much, a lot ,far　等

③ 稍微；作定语或状语

a little, a bit ,somewhat, slightly, more or less 等

④ 大小

predominantly	主要（地）
to a less(slight) degree(extent)	在较小程度上
in a greater degree	在较大程度上
in a considerable degree	在很大程度上
to a high degree	在很高程度上
to a certain extent	在某种程度上
in some degree	在某种程度上

⑤ 粗细

at large	笼统地
in detail, in full length	详细地
in a more detailed fashion	更为详细地
in considerable detail	相当详细地
in more detail	比较详细地
in some detail	较为详细地

⑥ 范围

Radically	根本上
on the whole	总的说来，大体上
in general, far and by	大体上，一般说来
essentially, basically, primarily, largely	基本上
main, chief, primary, major	主要的（定语）
mostly, mainly, chiefly, dominantly	主要的，大部分
predominantly, in the main ,in a great measure	主要地，大部分
for the most part, for the greater part	主要地，大部分
entirely, completely, utterly, wholly, to the full extent	完全地
in part, partially, partly	部分地
extremely, in the extreme, to the last degree	极其，非常

⑦ 度量

on the order of	相当于……数量，大约
to within	……在……精度以内
by weight(volume, area…)	按重量（体积、面积）计量
a slope of …in (on ,to)	……坡度
a batter of…in	……斜度
angle of… with	与……成……角

at an angle of θ to	……与……成θ角
an a right angle to ,squared to	与……成直角
in length (width, depth…)	按长度（宽度、深度、……）
数学+单位+long(wide, deep…)	长（宽、深……）……

【例 37】 Table 2.2 gives an indication of the typical range of constituents in SCC by weight and by volume.

【例 38】 On the whole, the bulk density of slowly cooled slags, which typically ranges from 1120 to 1360 kg/m^3, is some-where between normal-weight natural aggregate and structural lightweight aggregate.

【例 39】 The rheology of fresh concrete can be mainly described by its yield point and plastic viscosity:

（7）Scale and Rate（Proportion and Ratio）比例和比率

在 Uint 2 中，曾论述过数的增减速、比较和倍数等表达，这里再介绍数的比率和比例的一般表达方式。常用语句结构如下。

① {
be a direct measure of
be a direct dependence upon (on)
vary (directly)as
vary in the direct ratio of   与……成正比例
be(directly)proportional to
be in proportion to
be relative to
}

② …(be)in the proportion of …   与……成比例

③ {
be in relation to
be an inverse measure of
be an inverse dependence upon(on)
vary inversely as
vary in the inverse ratio of
vary in the reciprocal of   与……成反比例
be inversely proportional to
be in inverse proportion to
depend(s)inversely as
}

【例 40】 The mass transfer coefficient (DCT) is proportional to the flux of theliquid.

【例 41】 For mild steel loaded in elastic region, the stress varies directly as strain

（8）Tables and Graph（Diagram）and Fomula 图表与公式

在科技论文中，为了更加直观、简洁和明确表述一定的概念、理论和应用，往往采用不少图表和公式。

① 图　与图有关的词汇有：graph, diagram, drawing, chart, sketch 等，如：

curve line graph　（曲线图）

projection drawing（投影图）

40

flow chart （流程图）

diagrammatic sketch （示意图）

key diagram （概略原理图）

perspective drawing （透视图）

histogram （直方图，频率曲线）

在工程图纸中常用的词汇：plan（平面图）、side view（侧视图）、top view（俯视图）、elevation（立面图）、section（截面图）、detail（大样图）、scale（比例）等。

若论文较短，可将文中所有的图形按顺序依次编号，如：Fig.1,Fig.2,……对于较长的学位论文或报告，可分章节编号，如 Fig.1-1,Fig.1-2,…或 Fig.1.1,Fig.1.2，等；图名跟在其后。另外，若采用的图形引自其他文献，就需要在文中或图名后注明来源。

【例 42】 As can be seen in Tables 9.2 and 9.3 and Figure 9.1, aluminous cements definitely have chemical and phase compositions that are completely different from those of Portland cement.

注明来源的方式有以下几种：

source:Ellingwood,1977 （资料来源：……）

photograph, H. L. Smith（图片取自……）

Furnished by permission of...（蒙……允许载用）

Courtesy of the...（蒙……特许刊用）

From: ... published by...（引用……出版的……）

copyright,...（本图版权为……所有）

【例 43】 As indicated in Fig.2,stress intensity is shown on the vertical axis and strain on the horizontal.

在论文中，有时还需要对图形中的符号及其位置等进行解释。举例如下。

at the top 在顶上

at the bottom right 在右下角

at the top left 在左上角

in the middle 在中间

upper(middle, lower)part （一张图的）上（中、下）部

upper (lower)half （一张图的）上（下）一半

top (bottom)row 上（下）一排

top (middle, bottom, right, left)panel(plot) 指图（figure）中某一小（分）图的位置

blackened(full, filled, solid)circle 实心圆

open circle 空心圆　line of circles 圆点组成的线

(solid, open)square （实心、空心）方块

cross 十字符号

dashed line (chain dash) 小线段（虚线）

dash-dot-dash line 一·一 线

chain dot 点线(.....)

dotted-dashed line 点划线

(solid, broken)line （实、虚）线

heavy (thick)solid line 粗实线

thin(light)broken line 细虚线

(straight, wavy)line（直、波状）线

(smooth, dotted)curve（平滑、点）曲线

(shaded, clear)area（阴影、空白）区

(dotted, hatched, cross-hatched)area（布点、网状、阴影线）区

(dark, light)shaded area（深、线）阴影区

② 表　与表有关的词汇有：table、form、list 等。表的编号、标题的位置以及对表的来源的说明等与图的类似。注意，英语的表格一般只列横线，尽量少列竖线，几乎没有斜线。当一页不能容纳下一张表时，则在当页下注明 to be continued 并在下页上注明 continued。另外，对表中项目的注释，可放在表中，也可放在表外。

在解释表格内容时，会论及 row（行）、column（列）等，例如：

two rows from top	前两行
the middle row	中间 1 行
the third column from right	右数第 3 列
the second row from bottom	倒数第 2 行

③ 公式　公式或方程在科技论文中比比皆是。如同图表编号，公式的编号可按顺序依次进行，或按章节分开进行，其位置一般在公式的右侧靠边。下面给出若干描述公式推导的例子和相关词汇。

【例 44】 Assuming that… ,the solution takes the from…

其中，可用 by setting (putting, letting)…. 替代 Assuming that …, 与 take 相近的词有：result in 、yield、give、get、have 、arrive at、find、obtain、produce、follow 等。

【例 45】 By analogy to Eq.(2)the equation can be rewritten in the form of …

其中 by analogy to (by analogy with, on the analogy of)表示"根据…类推"。in the form(of the form, in …form)表示"以…形式"，如

in linear form	以线性形式
in equation form	以方程形式
in finite –difference form	以有限差分形式
in symbolic form	以符号形式
in nondimensional form	以无量纲形式
in integral form	以积分形式
in vectorial form	以矢量形式

【例 46】Additional details related to Eqs. (3.12 to 3.16) and examples can be found in [38].

【例 47】 Combining Eq. (1) and (2) allows us to write the expression for stress $\sigma = xyz$.

推导方程时常用到以下短语：

(by) substituting… into…

(by) inserting…

(by)eliminating… in…

42

(by)combining.. and…

(by)introducing… into…

(by)multiplying (dividing)…by…

subtracting(adding)…

(by)solving

(by)neglecting (ignoring, dropping)…

【例 48】 Where(in which)x refers to…, y is … and z=…

若需要对公式中的数学符号进行解释和定义，应在公式下一行起头处，用 where 或 in which （式中）引出。

【例 49】 Eqs.(5)-(6) were performed on initial conditions that…

常用的相关词汇有：perform、proceed、derive、simplification、approximation、(re)arrangement、algebra（代数运算）、positive、negative、 condition、assumption 等。

（9）Quantity and Unit 数量和单位

① 对数量的描述

【例 50】 Perlite is obtained when heating a rhyolitic rock which is transformed into a spongy mass that absorbs a lot of water.

描述数量、次数等的短语有：

a lot of ,lots of ,a great many	许多
a large quantity of, a great deal of	许多
a negligible amount of	很少一点
an insufficient quantity of	量不大的
a wide variety of	各种各样的
a mass of ,a volume of ,a world of	大量的
a series of ,a train of	一系列的

【例 51】 PNS is a brown liquid having a total solid content of about 40 to 41 per cent.

描述数量大小、近似、范围等的短评和词汇有：

about ,around ,some ,roughly, approximately	大约
in the vicinity of ,a matter of ,in the neighborhood of	大约
of(in, on)the order of	大约
order of magnitude	量级
range from … to…, in the range of…	在…范围内变化
up to…	最大（高、多、……）达……
down to…	最小（低、少、……）达……
as high (low, many, few)as …	高（低、多、少、……）达……
in excess of ,over ,above ,more (greater, higher)than	超过，……以上
below, under ,less (fewer)than	低于，……以下
increase (differ, decrease, change)by…	增在（相差、减小、变化）……

② 度量衡和单位换算 在写作中，常常会用到度量衡和单位换算。一般在论文中采用以下两种方式处理：一是用两种度量标注数量，如 2.5kip/ft （36.5KN/m）；二是采用一

种单位制，但在论文中或附录中列出所用到单位换算。土木工程常用的度量衡和单位换算见附录3。

③ 单位的表达　在英语中，"以……为单位"为 in unit of …或 in… ,by …。例如：

an angle in radians	以弧度为单位的角
weight in tons	质量以吨计
vehicle's speed in m/s	车速的单位为 m/s
by weight(volume, area)	以质量（体积、面积）计

当以数量词为单位时，采用"in＋基数词的复数"形式，如：

in hundreds	以百个为单位
in thousands	以千个为单位
in dozens	以打为单位
in millions of US dollars	以百万美元为单位

（10）NormalWords and Phrases 常用词汇

调查与研究：investigate, inquire, explore, examine, look into, inspect, study, consider, search, seek, seek out, analysis 等。

设计与准备：design, scheme, project, plan, propose, arrange, dispose, organize 等。

实验与试验：experiment, test, trial, try out, measure, record, equipment 等。

处理与操作：Examine, deal with, handle, treat, process, sort out, operate, conduct, activate, control, manage, function 等。

举例和例外：example, instance, case, illutration, exception, exclusion 等。

极值和均值：maximum, upper（上限），minimum, lower（下限），average 等。

准确和精确：accurate（准确），precise（精确），correct（正确），exact 等。

Part II Collections of English Literatures about Building Material

Unit 1   Classification of Materials

Basic Classifications and Engineering Materials

Solid materials have been conveniently grouped into three basic classifications: metals, ceramics, and polymers. This scheme is based primarily on chemical makeup and atomic structure, and most materials fall into one distinct grouping or another, although there are some intermediates. In addition, there are three other groups of important engineering materials-composites, semiconductors, and biomaterials. Composites consist of combinations of two or more different materials, whereas semiconductors are utilized because of their unusual electrical characteristics; biomaterials are implanted into the human body. A brief explanation of the material types and representative characteristics is offered next.

METALS: Metallic materials are normally combinations of metallic elements. They have large numbers of nonlocalized electrons; that is, these electrons are not bound to particular atoms. Many properties of metals are directly attributable to these electrons. Metals are extremely good conductors of electricity and heat and are not transparent to visible light; a polished metal surface has a lustrous appearance. Furthermore, metals are quite strong, yet deformable, which accounts for their extensive use in structural applications.

CERAMICS: Ceramics are compounds between metallic and nonmetallic elements; they are most frequently oxides, nitrides, and carbides. The wide range of materials that falls within this classification includes ceramics that are composed of clay minerals, cement, and glass. These materials are typically insulative to the passage of electricity and heat, and are more resistant to high temperatures and harsh environments than metals and polymers. With regard to mechanical behavior, ceramics are hard but very brittle.

POLYMERS: Polymers include the familiar plastic and rubber materials. Many of them are organic compounds that are chemically based on carbon, hydrogen, and other nonmetallic elements; furthermore, they have very large molecular structures. These materials typically have low densities and may be extremely flexible.

COMPOSITES: A number of composite materials have been engineered that consist of

45

more than one material type. Fiberglass is a familiar example, in which glass fibers are embedded within a polymeric material. A composite is designed to display a combination of the best characteristics of each of the component materials. Fiberglass acquires strength from the glass and flexibility from the polymer. Many of the recent material developments have involved composite materials.

SEMICONDUCTORS: Semiconductors have electrical properties that are intermediate between the electrical conductors and insulators. Furthermore, the electrical characteristics of these materials are extremely sensitive to the presence of minute concentrations of impurity atoms, which concentrations may be controlled over very small spatial regions. The semiconductors have made possible the advent of integrated circuitry that has totally revolutionized the electronics and computer industries (not to mention our lives) over the past two decades.

BIOMATERIALS: Biomaterials are employed in components implanted into the human body for replacement of diseased or damaged body parts. These materials must not produce toxic substances and must be compatible with body tissues (i.e., must not cause adverse biological reactions). All of the above materials-metals, ceramics, polymers, composites, and semiconductors-may be used as biomaterials. For example, in Section 20.8 are discussed some of the biomaterials that are utilized in artificial hip replacements.

Advanced Materials

Materials that are utilized in high-technology (or high-tech) applications are sometimes termed *advanced materials*. By high technology we mean a device or product that operates or functions using relatively intricate and sophisticated principles; examples include electronic equipment (VCRs, CD players, etc.), computers, fiberoptic systems, spacecraft, aircraft, and military rocketry. These advanced materials are typically either traditional materials whose properties have been enhanced or newly developed, high-performance materials. Furthermore, they may be of all material types (e.g., metals, ceramics, polymers), and are normally relatively expensive. In subsequent chapters are discussed the properties and applications of a number of advanced materials—for example, materials that are used for lasers, integrated circuits, magnetic information storage, liquid crystal displays (LCDs), fiber optics, and the thermal protection system for the Space Shuttle Orbiter.

Modern Materials' Needs

In spite of the tremendous progress that has been made in the discipline of materials science and engineering within the past few years, there still remain technological challenges, including the development of even more sophisticated and specialized materials, as well as consideration of the environmental impact of materials production. Some comment is appropriate relative to these issues so as to round out this perspective.

Nuclear energy holds some promise, but the solutions to the many problems that remain will necessarily involve materials, from fuels to containment structures to facilities for the disposal of radioactive waste.

Significant quantities of energy are involved in transportation. Reducing the weight of transportation vehicles (automobiles, aircraft, trains, etc.), as well as increasing engine operating temperatures, will enhance fuel efficiency. New high strength, low-density structural materials remain to be developed, as well as materials that have higher-temperature capabilities, for use in engine components.

Furthermore, there is a recognized need to find new, economical sources of energy, and to use the present resources more efficiently. Materials will undoubtedly play a significant role in these developments. For example, the direct conversion of solar into electrical energy has been demonstrated. Solar cells employ some rather complex and expensive materials. To ensure a viable technology, materials that are highly efficient in this conversion process yet less costly must be developed.

Additionally, environmental quality depends on our ability to control air and water pollution. Pollution control techniques employ various materials. In addition, materials processing and refinement methods need to be improved so that they produce less environmental degradation, that is, less pollution and less despoilage of the landscape from the mining of raw materials. Also, in some materials manufacturing processes, toxic substances are produced, and the ecological impact of their disposal must be considered.

Many materials that we use are derived from resources that are nonrenewable, that is, not capable of being regenerated. These include polymers, for which the prime raw material is oil, and some metals. These nonrenewable resources are gradually becoming depleted, which necessitates: 1) the discovery of additional reserves, 2) the development of new materials having comparable properties with less adverse environmental impact, and/or 3) increased recycling efforts and the development of new recycling technologies. As a consequence of the economics of not only production but also environmental impact and ecological factors, it is becoming increasingly important to consider the "cradle-to-grave" life cycle of materials relative to the overall manufacturing process.

New Word and Expressions

intermediate	adj.	中间的；n. 媒介，中间品
ceramic	n.	陶瓷，陶瓷制品
polymer	n.	聚合物，聚合体，聚合材料
composite	n.	复合物，复合体，复合材料
semiconductor	n.	半导体，半导体材料
biomaterial	n.	生物材料
implant	n.	移植，植入
oxide	n.	氧化物
nitride	n.	氮化物
carbide	n.	碳化物
brittle	adj.	脆的，易碎的
recycle	n. & vt.	（使）再循环，再利用，回收

transparent	adj.	透明的，显然的，明晰的
lustrous	adj.	有光泽的，光辉的
impurity	n.	杂质，混杂物，不洁，不纯
circuitry	n.	电路，线路
despoil	vt.	夺取，掠夺
renewable	adj.	可更新的，可恢复的

Exercises

1. Translate the following sentences from English into Chinese.

(1) Metallic materials are normally combinations of metallic elements. They have large numbers of nonlocalized electrons; that is, these electrons are not bound to particular atoms. Many properties of metals are directly able to these electrons.

(2) Ceramics are compounds between metallic and nonmetallic elements; they are most frequently oxides, nitrides, and carbides. The wide range of materials that falls within this classification includes ceramics that are composed of clay minerals, cement, and glass.

(3) Polymers include the familiar plastic and rubber materials. Many of them are organic compounds that are chemically based on carbon, hydrogen, and other nonmetallic elements; furthermore, they have very large molecular structures. These materials typically have low densities and may be extremely flexible.

(4) A composite is designed to display a combination of the best characteristics of each of the component materials. Fiberglass acquires strength from the glass and flexibility from the polymer. Many of the recent material developments have involved composite materials.

2. Translate the following sentences from Chinese into English.

(1) 金属材料通常由金属元素组成。它们有大量无规则运动的电子。也就是说，这些电子不是被约束于某个特定原子的。

(2) 这些半导体使得集成电路的出现变得可能，在过去 20 多年间，这些集成电路革新了电子装置和计算机工业。

(3) 生物材料被应用于移植进入人类身体以取代病变的或者损坏的身体部件。这些材料不能产生有毒物质而且必须同人的身体器官相容（比如，不能导致相反的生物反应）。

(4) 除此之外，寻找新的、经济的能源资源，并且更加有效地使用现存的资源被公认是必需的。材料将毫无疑问地在这些发展过程中扮演重要的角色。

Unit 2　Cement Science

Classification of Cements

Cements can be divided into the following categories:

1. Portland cements which can be subdivided into:

(a) Ordinary Portland cement;

(b) Rapid hardening Portland cement;

(c) Extra rapid hardening Portland cement;

(d) Portland blast-furnace cement;

(e) Low heat Portland cement;

(f) Sulphate resisting Portland cement;

(g) White Portland cement;

(h) Colored Portland cement.

2. Natural cement.

3. High alumina cement.

4. Supersulphated cement.

5. Special cements.

(a) Masonry cement;

(b) Trass cement;

(c) Expansive cement;

(d) Oil well cement;

(e) Jet set cement;

(f) Hydrophobic cement;

(g) Waterproof cement.

American Types of Cement

In America Portland cements are divided under the ASTM (American Society for Testing Materials) Standards into the following types:

Type Ⅰ :For use in general concrete construction where the special properties specifies=d for types Ⅱ, Ⅲ, Ⅳ and Ⅴ are not required.

Type Ⅱ: For use in general concrete construction exposed to moderate heart of hydration is required.

Type Ⅲ: For use when high early strength is required.

Type Ⅳ: For use when low heart of hydration is required.

Type Ⅴ: For use when high sulphate resistance is required.

In addition, there are Type Ⅰ A, Ⅱ A and Ⅲ A which are exactly the same as Types Ⅰ, Ⅱ, and Ⅲ except that thy have an airentraining agent added.

The Manufacture and Delivery of Portland Cement

The principal raw materials used in the manufacture of cement are:

1. Argillaceous or silicates of aluminum in the form of clays and shales.

2. Calcareous, or calcium carbonate, in the form of limestone, chalk and marl which is a mixture of clay and calcium carbonate.

The ingredients are mixed very roughly in the proportion of two parts of calcareous material to one part of argillaceous material. Limestone and shales have first to be crushed. They may the be ground in ball mills in a dry state or mixed in a wet state, the latter being preferable for the softer types of raw material and most commonly used by British manufacturers as it permits more accurate control of the ultimate composition. The dry powder, or in the case of the wet process the slurry, is then burnt in a rotary kiln at a temperature between 1400℃ to 1500℃, pulverized coal, gas or oil being used as the fuel. In the wet process the chemical composition of the slurry can easily be checked and if necessary corrected before it is passed into the kiln.

The clinker obtained from the kilns is first cooled and then passed on to ball mills where gypsum is added and it is ground to the product is generally stored in silos at the works before dispatch, but in terms of shortage it may be sent to the user straight from the mills, in which case it will still be hot when used. This has led to considerable controversy and hot cement has often rejected by the user. In fact, cement in a hot state can normally be used quite satisfactorily, as the aggregate and water is sufficient in bulk to reduce the temperature quickly to a safe value. Cement can be sent to the user in bulk containers or can be packed in drums jute sacks or multiply paper bags, the last now being favored in British practice.

In British practice a bag of cement weighs 1 cwt (112 1b) giving 20 bags to the ton. In American practice a bag of cement contains 94 1b of cement giving 24 bags to the ton and a barrel contains 376 1b of cement giving 6 barrels to the ton.

Cement is normally assumed to weigh 90 1b per cu ft, although 82 1b per cu ft is perhaps a better average figure. It may weigh between 75 and 110 1b per cu ft according to its state of compaction. According to the ASTM specifications, cements which have been stored after testing and before deliver for more than 6 months in bulk or 3 months if in bags may be retested before use.

Compound Composition of Portland Cement

The constituents forming the raw materials used in the manufacture of Portland cements combine to form compounds in the finished product, the following being the most important. These compounds have been called Bogue compounds as it is largely due to him that they have been identified.

Compound	Chemical	Usual abbreviated designation
Tricalcium silicate	$3CaO \cdot SiO_2$	C_3S
Dicalcium silicate	$2CaO \cdot SiO_2$	C_2S
Tricalcium aluminate	$3CaO \cdot Al_2O_3$	C_3A
Tetracalcium alumino-ferrite	$4CaO \cdot Al_2O_3 \cdot Fe_2O_3$	C_4AF

Bogue and others have given formulae by which the compound composition of cement can be calculated from the chemical analysis of the raw materials and the formulae adopted by the American Society for Testing Materials (ASTM) are as follows:

Amount of tricalcium silicate per cent

$=(4.07\times$per cent CaO$) - (7.06\times$Per Cent SiO$_2) - (6.72\times$per cent Al$_2$O$_3)$

$-(1.43\times$per cent Fe$_2$O$_3) - (2.85\times$per cent SO$_3)$

Amount of dicalcium silicate per cent

$=(2.87\times$per cent SiO$_2) - (0.754\times$per cent 3CaO·SiO$_2)$

Amount of tricalcium aluminate per cent

$=(2.65\times$per cent Al$_2$O$_3) - (1.69\times$per cent Fe$_2$O$_3)$

Amount of tetracalcium alumino-ferrite per cent

$=3.04\times$per cent Fe$_2$O$_3$

In addition, there may be present small amounts of gypsum, magnesium oxide, free lime and silicate in the form of glass.

A liquid is formed at the burning temperature and this contains, in addition to other compounds, all the alumina and iron oxide present in the cement. The alumina and iron compounds present in the cement are formed by crystallization of this liquid on cooling. Some of the liquid may however form glass according to the conditions in the kiln and the quantity of alumina and iron compounds formed will depend on the extent of this action. Variations in the kilning process therefore affect the properties of the cement. If glass is formed the quantities of alumina and iron compounds present will be reduced.

The C$_3$S and C$_2$S constituents form 70 to 80 per cent of all Portland cements, are the most stable and contribute most to the eventual strength and resistance of the concrete to corrosive salts, alkalis and acids. The C$_3$S hydrates more rapidly than the C$_2$S and it therefore contributes more to the early strength and the heat generated and therefore the rise in temperature. The contribution of the C$_2$S to strength takes principally within the first 24 hours and is the least stable of the four principal components of the cement. The C$_4$AF component is comparatively inactive and contributes little at any age to the strength or heat of hydration of the cement. It is more stable than the C$_3$A component but less stable than the C$_3$A and C$_2$S. The presence of glass increases the early strength and the heat generated. The C$_3$A is liable to decompose to hydroxides of calcium and aluminum on exposure to air and water and the ease with which it is attacked by salts and alkalis renders its presence undesirable for any hydraulic or marine works. The rates of heat evolution of the four principal compounds, if equal amounts are considered, would be in the following order: C$_3$A, C$_3$S, C$_4$AF and C$_2$S.

The difference in the properties of the various kinds of Portland cement arises from the relative proportion of the four principal compounds they possess and from the fineness to which the cement clinker is ground. Thus rapid hardening Portland cement is ground finer than and may possess more C$_3$S and less C$_2$S than ordinary Portland cement. The difference for any one works is usually in the fineness of grinding. Sulphate resisting cement is characterized by an exceptionally low percentage of C_3A and low heat cement should have a low percentage of C_3A and relatively more C_2S and less C_3S than ordinary Portland cement; it will therefore have a low rate gain of strength.

The compound compositions of cements of different manufacturers and in different countries can vary widely but an approximate idea of the relative proportions of the various compounds in the different kinds of Portland cement according to Lea is given in Table 2-1.

Table 2-1 Composition and compound of Portland cement (After Lea)

Analysis: percent	Rapid hardening	Normal	Low-heat	Sulphate resisting
Lime	64.5	63.1	60.0	64.0
Silica	20.7	20.6	22.5	24.4
Alumina	5.2	6.3	5.2	3.7
Iron oxide	2.9	3.6	4.6	3.0
Compounds: percent				
Tricalcium silicate	50	40	25	40
Dicalcium silicate	21	30	45	40
Tricalcium aluminate	9	11	6	5
Iron compound	9	11	14	9

The salient point demonstrated by this table is the comparatively large variation in compound composition that can apply even with a very small variation in the chemical analysis of the raw materials.

Summary of Properties of the Principal Cements

The properties of cements can be summarized as in Table 2-2 which is due to Lea.

Table 2-2 Properties of different cements

	Rate of strength Development	Rate of heat evolution	Drying shrinkage	Resistance to cracking	Inherent resistance to chemical deterioration
Portland cements					
Rapid-hardening	High	High	Medium	Low	Low
Normal	Medium	Medium	Medium	Medium	Low
Low-heat	Low	Low	Somewhat higher	High	Medium
Sulphate-resisting	Low to medium	Low to medium	Medium	Medium	High
Cements containing blast-furnace slag					
Portland	b.-f.slag	Medium	Medium	Medium	Medium
Supersulphate	Medium	Very low	Medium	Inadequate Information	High
High alumina cement	Very high	Very high	Medium	Low	Very high
Pozzolanic cements	Low	Low to medium	Somewhat higher	High	High

New Word and Expressions

subdivide	v.	细分，细区分，再划分
hydrophobic	adj.	憎水的
blast-furnace	n.	高炉，鼓风炉
trass	n.	[矿]火山灰，粗面凝灰岩
supersulphated	adj.	富硫酸盐的，过硫化的
jet	n.	射流，喷气，喷射
oil well		油井
waterproof	adj.	防水的，不透水的
alumina	n.	矾土，铝氧土，氧化铝
sulphate	n.	硫酸盐
masonry	n.	砖石建筑，砌砖，砌块
air entraining agent		加气剂，引气剂
argillaceous	adj.	泥质的，含黏土的
clinker	n.	水泥熟料，渣块
pulverize	v.	研磨成粉
clay	n.	黏土
gypsum	n.	石膏
shale	n.	页岩，油页岩
requisite	adj.	必要的，所需要的
calcareous	adj.	含钙的，石灰质的
drum	n.	转筒，滚筒
calcium carbonate		碳酸钙
jute sack		黄麻袋，麻布袋
limestone	n.	石灰石
barrel	n.	筒
chalk	n.	白垩，碳酸钙
cwt	Abbr.	等于 hundredweight 英担（1/20吨，英制为112磅，美制为100磅）
marl	n.	泥灰石，泥灰岩
tricalcium	n.	三钙
ingredient	n.	成分，组成成分，配料
tricalcium silicate		硅酸三钙
dicalcium	n.	二钙
roughly	adv.	概略地，粗糙地
tetracalcium	n.	四钙
ball mill		球磨机
dicalcium silicate		硅酸二钙
slurry	n.	泥浆
aluminate	n.	铝酸盐
aluminoferrite	n.	铁铝酸盐
kiln	n.	窑，炉；vt. 烧窑，在干燥炉中使……干燥
rotary cement kiln		回转式水泥窑

53

formulae	n.	公式，算式
magnesium	n.	镁（Mg）
marine	adj.	海的，海产的
salient	adj.	显著的，突出的，卓越的
crystallization	n.	结晶
lime	n.	生石灰，石灰
alkali	n.	碱，强碱
corrosive	adj.	侵蚀的，腐蚀性的
silica	n.	硅石，二氧化硅,氧化硅
hydrate	v.	与水化合，水化
inherent	adj.	固有的，先天的
decompose	n.	分解 v.分解
deterioration	n.	退化，变质
aluminum	n.	铝
slag	n.	矿渣，熔渣
hydraulic	adj.	水力的，用水的
pozzolanic	adj.	火山灰质的

Exercises

1. Translate the following sentences from English into Chinese.

(1) The principal raw materials used in the manufacture of cement are:

① Argillaceous or silicates of aluminum in the form of clays and shales;

② Calcareous calcium carbonate, in the form of limestone, chalk and marl which is a mixture of clay and calcium carbonate.

(2) They may then be ground in ball mills in a dry state or mixed in a wet state, the latter being preferable for the softer types of raw material and most commonly used by British manufactures as it permits more accurate control of the ultimate composition.

(3) In the wet process the chemical composition of the slurry can easily be checked and if necessary corrected before it is passed into the kiln.

(4) The finished product is generally stored in silos at the works before dispatch, but in terms of shortage it may be sent to the user straight from the mills, in which case it will still be hot when used.

2. Translate the following sentences from Chinese into English.

(1) 在英国的工程应用中，每袋水泥约重 1 英担（112 磅），20 袋水泥为一吨；而在美国，每袋水泥重 94 磅，24 袋水泥为一吨，或者每桶水泥 376 磅，6 桶为一吨。

(2) 用于制造波兰特水泥的各种原料在炉窑内相互反应，并最终形成水泥的各种熟料。

(3) 伯格（Bogue）及其他研究人员推导出了若干计算公式，利用这些公式，人们可根据水泥原料的化学成分分析结果，计算出水泥熟料中化合物的组成。该公式已被美国材料实验协会采用。

(4) 硅酸三钙和硅酸二钙占各种波兰特水泥熟料组分的 70%～80%，是水泥熟料中最重要的组成部分，因而对混凝土的最终强度及抵抗酸、碱和盐的腐蚀能力起着重要作用。

(5) 按等量计算，波兰特水泥熟料中四种主要化合物水化热释放率的大小顺序为：C_3A、C_3S、C_4AF 和 C_2S。

Unit 3   Concrete Science

Introduction

Concrete is a man-made composite, the major constituent of which is natural aggregates, such as gravel and sand or crushed rock. Alternatively artificial aggregates, for example, blast-furnace slag, expanded clay, broken brick and steel shot may be used where appropriate. The other principal constituent of concrete is the binding medium used to bind the aggregate particles together to form a hard composite material. The most commonly used binding medium is the product formed by a chemical reaction between cement and water. Other binding mediums are used on a much smaller scale for special concretes in which the cement and water of normal concretes are replaced either wholly or in part by epoxide or polyester resins. These polymer concretes known as resin-based or resin-additive concretes respectively are costly and generally not suitable for use where fire-resistant properties are required, but they are useful for repair work and other special applications. Resin-based concretes have been used, for example, for pre-cast chemical-resistant pipes and light-weight drainage channels.

In its hardened state concrete is a rock-like material with a high compressive strength. By virtue of the ease with which fresh concrete in its plastic state may be moulded into virtually any shape, it may be used to advantage architecturally or solely for decorative purposes. Special surface finishes, for example, exposed aggregate, can also be used to great effect.

Normal concrete has a comparatively low tensile strength and for structural applications it is normal practice either to incorporate steel bars to resist any tensile forces (reinforced concrete) or to apply compressive forces to the concrete to counteract these tensile forces (prestressed concrete). Concrete is also used in conjunction with other materials, for example, it may form the compression flange of a box section the remainder of which is steel (composite construction). Concrete is used structurally in buildings for foundations, columns, beams and slabs, in shell structures, bridges, sewage-treatment works, railway sleeps, roads, cooling towers, dams, chimneys, harbors, off-shore structures, coastal protection works, and so on. It is used also for a wide range of pre-cast concrete products, which include concrete blocks, cladding panels, pipes and lamps standards.

The impact strength, as well as the tensile strength, of normal concretes is low and this can be improved by the introduction of randomly orientated fibers into the concrete mix. Steel, polypropylene, asbestos and glass fibers have all been used with some success in pre-cast products, for example, pipes, building panels and piles. Steel fibers also increase the flexural strength or modulus of rupture of concrete and this particular type of fiber-reinforced concrete has been used in ground paving slabs for roads where flexural and impact strength are both important. Fiber-reinforced concretes are however essentially special-purpose concretes and for most purposes the normal concretes described in this lesson are used.

In addition to its potential from aesthetic considerations, concrete require little maintenance and has good fire resistance. Concrete has other properties that may on occasions be considered less desirable, for example, the time-dependent deformations associated with drying shrinkage and other related phenomena. However, if the effects of environmental conditions, creep, shrinkage and loading on the dimensional changes of concrete structures and structural elements are fully appreciated, and catered for at the design stage, no subsequent difficulties in this respect should arise.

A true appreciation of the relevant properties of any material is necessary if a satisfactory end product is to be obtained and concrete, in the respect, is no different from other materials.

Constituent Materials

Concrete is composed mainly of three materials, namely, cement, water and aggregate, and an additional material, known as an admixture, is sometimes added to modify certain of its properties. Cement is the chemically active constituent but its reactivity is only brought into effect on mixing with water. The aggregate plays no part in chemical reactions but its usefulness arises because it is an economical filler material with good resistance to volume changes, which take place within the concrete after mixing, and it improves the durability of the concrete.

A typical structure of hardened concrete and the proportions of the constituent materials encountered in most concrete mixes are shown in Figure 3-1. In a properly proportioned and compacted concrete the voids are usually less than 2 per cent. The properties of concrete in its fresh and hardened state can be shown large variations depending on the type, quality and proportions of the constituents and from the following discussion students should endeavor to appreciate the significance of those properties of the constituent materials which affect concrete behavior.

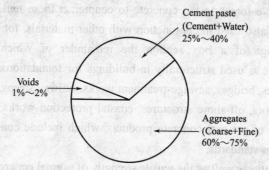

Figure 3-1　Composition of concrete

Cement

The different cements used for making concrete are finely ground powders and all have the important property that when mixed with water a chemical reaction (hydration) takes place which, in time, produces a very hard and strong binding medium for the plastic state cement mortar gives to the fresh concrete its cohesive properties.

For the different types of cement, certain physical and chemical requirements are specified

56

in British Standards, methods of testing cement for various properties are described in BS 4450. Of these, ordinary Portland cement is the most widely used, the others being used where concrete with special properties are required.

Portland cement was developed in 1824 and derives its name from Portland limestone in Dorset because of its close resemblance to this rock after hydration has taken place. The basic raw materials used in the manufacture of Portland cements are calcium carbonate, found in calcareous rocks such as limestone or chalk, and silica, alumina and iron oxide found in argillaceous rocks such as clay or shale. Marl, which is a mixture of calcareous and argillaceous materials, can also be used.

Aggregate

Aggregate is much cheaper than cement and maximum economy is obtained by using as much aggregate as possible in concrete. Its use also considerably improves both the volume stability and the durability of the resulting concrete. The commonly held view that aggregate is completely inert filler in concrete is not true, its physical characteristics and in some cases its chemical composition affecting to a varying degree the properties of concrete in both its plastic and hardened states.

The criterion for a good aggregate is that it should produce the desired properties in both the fresh and hardened concrete. In testing aggregates it is important that a truly representative sample is used. The procedure for obtaining such a test sample is described in BS 812: Part 1.

The basic properties of the aggregate include physical properties, shape and surface texture and grading. The properties of the aggregate known to have a significant effect on concrete behavior are its strength, deformation, durability, toughness, hardness, volume change, porosity, relative density and chemical reactivity. The other types of the aggregate include heavyweight aggregate, lightweight aggregates, whose contribution is very small in comparison with rock aggregate. Heavyweight aggregates provide an effective and economical use of concrete for radiation shielding, by giving the necessary protection against X-rays, gamma rays and neutrons, and for weight coating of submerged pipelines. Lightweight aggregates find application in a wide variety of concrete products ranging from insulating screeds to reinforced or pre-stressed concrete although their greatest use has been in the manufacture of pre-cast concrete blocks.

Water

Water used in concrete, in addition to reacting with cement and thus causing it to set and harden, also facilitates mixing, placing and compacting of the fresh concrete. It is also used for washing the aggregates and for curing purposes. In general water fit for drinking, such as tap water, is acceptable for mixing concrete. The impurities that are likely to have an adverse effect when present in appreciable quantities include silt, clay, acids, alkalis and other salts, organic matter and sewage. The use of seawater does not appear to have any adverse effect on the strength and durability of Portland cement concrete but it is known to cause surface dampness, efflorescence and staining and should be avoided where concrete with a good appearance is required. Seawater also increases the risk of corrosion of steel and its use in reinforced concrete is not recommended. When the suitability of mixing water is in question, it is desirable to test for both the nature and extent of contamination as prescribed in BS 3148. The quality of water may also be assessed by comparing the setting time and soundness of cement pastes made with water of known quality and the water whose quality is suspect.

The use of impure water for washing aggregates can adversely affect strength and durability if it deposits harmful substances of the particles. In general, the presence of impurities in the curing water does not have any harmful effects, although it may spoil the appearance of concrete. Water containing appreciable amounts of acid or organic materials should be avoided.

Admixtures

Admixtures are substances introduced into a batch of concrete, during or immediately before its mixing, in order to alter or improve the properties of the fresh or hardened concrete or both. Although certain finely divided solids, such as pozzolanas and slags, fall within the above broad definition of admixtures, they are distinctly different from what is commonly regarded as the main steam of admixtures and therefore should be treaded separately. It should also be noted that the materials used by the cement manufactures to modify the properties of cement are normally described as additives.

In general, the changes brought about in the concrete by the use of admixtures are effected through the influence of the admixtures on hydration, liberation of heat, formation of pores and the development of the gel structure. Concrete admixtures should only be considered for use when the required modifications cannot be made by varying the composition and proportion of the basic constituent materials, or when the admixtures can produce the required effects more economically.

Since admixtures may also have detrimental effects, their suitability for a particular concrete should be carefully evaluated before use, based on a knowledge of their main active ingredients, on available performance data and on trial mixes. The specific effects of an admixture generally vary with the type of cement, mix composition, ambient conditions (particularly temperature) and its dosage. Since the quantity of admixture used is both small and critical, the required dose must be carefully determined and administered. Where related British Standard exist (BS 5075) the admixtures should comply with their specifications. It should be remembered that admixtures are not intended to replace good concreting practice and should not be used in discriminately.

New Words and Expressions

gravel	n.	砾石，卵石
finish	n.	表面光度，抛光，涂层
artificial	adj.	人工的，人造的
counteract	n.	反作用，平衡 vt. 抵消，中和
slag	n.	矿渣，熔渣

pre-stressed	adj.	预应力的，预拉伸的
shot	n.	丸，砂
flange	n.	凸缘，翼缘，法兰盘
epoxide	n.	环氧化合物，环氧衍生物
slab	n.	平板，铺石板，厚片
polyester	n.	聚酯
cladding	n.	路面，覆盖层，包层
resin	n.	树脂，树脂制品，胶质
polypropylene	n.	聚丙烯
pre-cast	vt.	预浇，预制，装配式
asbestos	n.	石棉
lightweight	adj.	轻的，重量轻的
flexural	adj.	弯曲的，挠性的
heavyweight	adj.	重的，特别重的
modulus	n.	模量，系量，模数
drainage	n.	排水，排水设备，排水管
paving	n.	铺路，铺砌，铺面材料
by[in] virtue of		靠……力量，由于
aesthetic	adj.	美术的，美学的
mould=mold	n.,vt.,vi.	模型，模板，铸造，铸模
time-dependent	adj.	时间决定的
drying shrinkage		干缩
gamma-ray	n.	伽马射线（γ射线）
shrinkage	n.	收缩量，收缩率，收缩
neutron	n.	中子
creep	n.	蠕变，徐变
submerged	adj.	浸（沉，淹）没的
cater	vi.(to, for)	迎合，投合
screed	n.	整平板，刮板
durability	n.	耐久性，寿命
silt	n.	泥沙，泥浆，粉砂，淤泥
plastic	adj.	可塑的，塑性的
adverse	adj.	逆的，不利的，相反的
elastic	adj.	弹性的
sewage	n.	污水，下水道，污水，废水，污物
cohesive	adj.	内聚的，黏合的
dampness	n.	潮湿，湿度，含水量
derive	vt.	推导；vi. 起源于
efflorescence	n.	风化，粉化
inter	adj.	惰性的，不活泼的
suitability	n.	适合，适用，适应性
criterion	n.	（评判的）标准，规范
contamination	n.	污染，污染物
texture	n.	结构，构造，织构，纹理

prescribe	n.	指定，规定；vt. 规定，开药方
porosity	n.	孔隙率，多孔性
prescribe	n.	指定，规定；vt. 规定，开药方
reactivity	n.	反应性，活性
cure	n.	硬化，养护
shield	n.	盾，保护，罩，防护，屏蔽
pozzolana=pozzuolana		火山灰（可作水泥原料）
pore	n.	孔隙，毛孔，气孔，孔
dosage	n.	剂量，配药
additive	n.	添加物，掺和料
discriminately	adv.	区别地，区别对待地
admixture	n.	外加剂
vary	vt,vi.	（1）改变，换，修改（2）（使）多样化，（使）变化
detrimental	adj.	有害的
trial mix		试拌
ambient	adj.	周围的；n. 周围环境
comply with		同意，答应;遵守，服从

Exercises

1. Translate the following sentences from English into Chinese.

(1) Concrete is composed mainly of three materials, namely, cement, water and aggregate, and an additional material, known as an admixture, is sometimes added to modify of its properties.

(2) By virtue of the ease with which fresh concrete in its plastic state may be moulded into virtually any shape, it may used to advantage architecturally or solely for decorative purposes.

(3) A typical structure of hardened concrete and the proportions of the constituent materials encountered in most concrete mixes are shown in figure 3-1. They include 1%~2% voids, 25%~40% cement paste and 60%~75% aggregates.

(4) The impact strength, as well as tensile strength, of normal concretes is low and this can be improved by the introduction of randomly orientated fibers into the concrete mix. Steel, polypropylene, asbestos and glass fibers have all been used with some success in pre-cast products.

2. Translate the following sentences from Chinese into English.

(1) 一些特殊的表面处理，例如将石子等粗骨料压入混凝土表面，能够获得非常好的艺术效果。

(2) 要想获得令人满意的产品，就必须了解所有材料的有关性能。在这方面，混凝土制品与其他材料制品是完全一样的。

(3) 在混凝土中水泥是具有化学活性的组分，但其反应活性只有在与水拌后才能表现出来。

(4) 人们认识到，对混凝土的性质有重大影响的骨料特性是：骨料的强度，性变能力，耐久性，韧性，硬度，体积稳定性，孔隙率，相对密度及化学活性。

60

Unit 4　High Performance Concretes (HPC)

Introduction

High performance concretes (HPC) are concretes with properties or attributes that satisfy the performance criteria. Generally concretes with higher strengths and attributes superior to conventional concretes are desirable in the construction industry. For the purpose of this article, HPC is defined in terms of strength and durability. The researchers of Strategic Highway Research Program SHRP-C-205 on High Performance Concrete defined the high performance concretes for pavement applications in terms of strength, durability attributes and water-cementitious materials ratio as follows:

- It shall have one of the following strength characteristics:

4-hour compressive strength≥2500 psi (17.5 MPa) termed as very early strength concrete (VES), or

24-hour compressive strength≥5000 psi (35MPa) termed as high early strength concrete (HES), or

28-day compressive strength≥10000 psi (70 MPa) termed as very high strength concrete (VHS).

- It shall have a durability factor greater than 80% after 300 cycles of freezing and thawing.

- It shall have a water-cementitious materials ratio≤0.35.

High strength concrete (HSC) could be considered as high performance if other attributes are satisfactory in terms of its intended application. Generally concretes with higher strengths exhibit superiority of other attributes. In American practice, high strength concrete is usually considered to be a concrete with a 28 days compressive strength of at least 6 000 psi (42 MPa). In a recent CEBFIB State of the Art Report on High Strength Concrete it is defined as concrete having a minimum 28 days compressive strength of 8 700 psi (60 MPa). Clearly then, the definition of "high strength concrete" is relative; it depends upon both the period of time in question, and the location.

The proportioning (or mix design) of normal strength concretes is based on primarily on the w/c ratio "law" first proposed by Abrams in 1918. At least for concretes with strengths up to 6000 psi (42 MPa), it is implicitly assumed that almost any normal-weight aggregates will be stronger than the hardened cement paste. There is thus no explicit consideration of aggregate strength (or elastic modulus) in the commonly used mix design procedures, such as those proposed by the American Concrete Institute. Similarly, the interfacial regions (or the cement-aggregate bond) are also not explicitly addressed. Rather, it is assumed that the strength of the hardened cement paste will be the limiting factor controlling the concrete strength.

61

For high strength concrete, however, all of the components of the concrete mixture are pushed to their critical limits. High strength concretes may be modeled as three-phase composite materials, the three phases being (i)the hardened cement paste (hcp); (ii) the aggregate; and (iii) the interfacial zone between the hardened cement paste and the aggregate. These three phases must all be optimized, which means that each must be considered explicitly in the design process. In addition, as has been pointed out by Mindess and Young.

It is necessary to pay careful attention to all aspects of concrete production (i.e. selection of materials, mix design, handling and placing). It cannot be emphasized too strongly that quality control is an essential part of the production of high-strength concrete and requires full cooperation among the material or ready-mixed supplier, the engineer, and the contractor.

In essence then, the proportioning of high strength concrete mixtures consists of three interrelated steps (1) selection of suitable ingredients-cement, supplementary cementing materials, aggregates, water and chemical mixtures, (2) determination of the relative quantities of these materials in order to produce, as economically as possible, a concrete that has the desired rheological properties, strength and durability (3) careful quality control of every phase of the concrete-making process.

Selection of Materials

As indicated above, it is necessary to get the maximum performance out of all of the materials involved in producing high strength concrete. For convenience, the various materials are discussed separately below. However, it must be remembered that prediction with any certainty as to how they will behave when combined in a concrete mixture is not feasible. Particularly when attempting to make high strength concrete, any material incompatibilities will be highly detrimental to the finished product. Thus, the culmination of any mix design process must be the extensive testing of trial mixes.

High strength concrete will normally contain not only Portland cement, aggregate and water, but also superplasticizers and supplementary cementing materials. It is possible to achieve compressive strengths of up to 14000 psi (98 MPa) using fly ash or ground granulated blast furnace slag as the supplementary cementing material. However, to achieve strengths in excess of 14000 psi (100 .Pa), the use of silica fume has been found to be essential, and it is frequently used for concretes in the strength range of 9000~14000 psi (63~98 MPa) as well.

Mix Proportions for High Strength Concrete

Only a few formal mix design methods for high strength concrete have been developed to date. Most commonly, purely empirical procedures based on trial mixtures are used. For instance, according to the Canadian Portland Cement Association, "the trial mix approach is best for selecting proportions for high-strength concrete". In other cases, mix design "recipes" are provided for different classes of high strength concrete.

Much work remains to be done before any mix proportioning method for high strength concrete becomes as universally accepted, at least in North America, as has the ACI Standard

211.1 for normal strength concretes.

In the end, as with conventional concrete, mix design will require the production of a number of trial mixes. In particular, it is essential first to ensure that the available raw materials are capable of producing the desired strengths, and that there are no incompatibilities between the cements, the admixtures and the supplementary cementing material. With materials for which there is not much field experience, it may be necessary to try different brands of cement, different brands of superplasticizers, and different sources of fly ash, slag, or silica fume, in order to optimize both the materials and the concrete mixture. This sounds like a lot of work, and in general it is. At present, there is simply no straightforward procedure for proportioning a high strength concrete mixture with unfamiliar materials.

Quality Control and Testing

Conventional normal strength concrete is a relatively forgiving material; it can tolerate small changes in materials, mix proportions or curing conditions without large changes in its mechanical properties. However, high strength concrete, in which all of the components of the mix are working at their limits, is not at all a forgiving material. Thus, to ensure the quality of high strength concrete, every aspect of the concrete production must be monitored, to form the uniformity of the raw materials to proper batching and mixing procedures, to proper transportation, placement, vibration and curing, through to proper testing of the hardened concrete.

The quality control procedures, such as the types of test on both the fresh and hardened concretes, the frequency of testing, and interpretation of test results are essentially the same as those for ordinary concrete. However, Cook has presented data which indicate that for his high strength concrete, the compressive strength results were not normally distributed, and the standard deviation for a given mix was not independent of test age and strength level. This led him to conclude that the "quality control techniques used for low to moderate strength concretes may not necessarily be appropriate for very high strength concretes." To this date, however, separate quality control/quality assurance procedures for high strength concrete have not been developed.

Conclusions

In conclusion, then, it has been shown that the production of high strength concrete requires careful attention to details. It also requires close cooperation between the owner, the engineer, the suppliers and producers of the raw materials, the contractor, and the testing laboratory. Perhaps the most important, we must remember that the well-known "law" and "rules-of-thumb" that apply to normal strength concrete may well not apply to high strength concrete, which is a distinctly different material. Nonetheless, we now know enough about high strength concrete to be able to produce it consistently, not only in the laboratory, but also in the field. It is to be hoped that codes of practice and testing standards catch up with the high strength concrete technology, so that the use of this exciting new material can continue to increase.

New Words and Expressions

superior	*adj.*	占优势的，胜过……的
interfacial	*adj.*	界面的，界面上的
in terms of		依据……，从……角度来讲
hardened cement paste		硬化水石泥
Strategic	*adj.*	战略的，战略上的，战略性的，关键性的
detrimental	*adj.*	有害的
optimize	*v.*	使最优化
cementitious	*adj.*	含水泥的，有黏结性的
interrelated	*adj.*	相互关联的
implicitly	*adj.*	含蓄的，暗中的
supplementary	*n.*	附加物，补充物，填补料；*adj.* 补充的，辅助的
explicit	*adj.*	明白的，显明的，直率的
rheological	*adj.*	【物】流变学的
address	*v.*	提出，表达，标注
feasible	*adj.*	可行的，切实可行的
incompatibility	*n.*	不相容性，不协调性
empirical	*adj.*	经验的经验主义的
culmination	*n.*	顶点，极度
recipe	*n.*	处方，制法，配方
fly ash		飞尘，飞灰，粉煤灰
brand	*n.*	商标，牌号，品种
granulated	*adj.*	颗粒状的
straightforward	*adj.*	直截了当的，直接的
blast furnace	*n.*	高炉，鼓风炉
interpretation	*n.*	解释，说明
silica fume		含硅烟雾，硅灰
forgiving	*adj.*	宽大的，仁慈的

Abbreviations

HPC=High Performance Concrete	高性能混凝土
VES=Very Early Strength Concrete	特早强混凝土
HES=High Early Strength Concrete	高早强混凝土
VHS=Very High Strength Concrete	特高强混凝土
HSC=High Strength Concrete	高强混凝土
ACI=American Concrete Institute	美国混凝土协会
CPCA=Canadian Portland Cement Association	加拿大水泥协会

Exercises

1. Translate the following sentences from English into Chinese.

(1) High strength concrete (HSC) could be considered as high performance if other attributes are satisfactory in terms of its intended application. Generally concretes with higher strengths exhibit

64

superiority of other attributes.

(2) For concretes with strength up to 6000 psi (42 MPa), it is implicitly assumed that almost any normal-weight aggregates will be stronger than the hardened cement paste.

(3) High strength concretes may be modeled as three-phase composite materials, the three phases being (i)the hardened cement paste (hcp), (ii) the aggregate, and (iii)the interfacial zone between the hardened cement paste and the aggregate.

(4) It must be remembered that prediction with any certainty as to how they will behave when combined in a concrete mixture is not feasible.

2. Translate the following sentences from Chinese into English.

(1) 经过 300 次冻融循环后，高性能混凝土仍具有大于 80%的耐久性系数。

(2) 在北美的工程实践中，通常认为高强混凝土是 28 天抗压强度至少为 6000 磅/英寸 ^{2} 的混凝土。

(3) 目前，还没有找到一种直接采用不熟悉的原料配制高强混凝土的程序。

(4) 高强混凝土除含有波特兰水泥、骨料和水外，还含有超塑化剂和水泥掺合料。

(5) 然而，时至今日，专门用于高强混凝土的独立质量控制体系尚未形成，相应的质量保证程序也未建立。

Unit 5　Admixtures

Introduction

An admixture is defined material other than water, aggregate, and hydraulic cement, which might be added to concrete before or during its mixing. This must not be confused with the term, addition, which is either inter-ground with or blended into a Portland cement during its manufacture. An addition is classified as being either (1) a processing addition, which aids in the manufacture and handing of the finished product, or (2) a functional addition, which modifies the use properties of the cement.

Admixture can function by several mechanisms.

1. Dispersing the cement in the aqueous phase of concrete.

2. Alteration of the normal rate of hydration of the cement, in particular the tricalcium silicate phase.

3. Reacting with the by-products of the hydrating cement, such as alkalis and calcium silicate hydroxide.

4. No reaction with either the cement or its by-products.

Those that function via the first two mechanisms are called chemical admixture in order to differentiate the others that perform by the last two mechanisms. The performance of chemical admixture is specified in ASTM C494.

Classification of Admixture

Admixtures may be classified as follows.

1. Water reducing chemical admixtures (WRAs)

This class of chemical admixtures permits the use of less water to obtain the same slump (a measure of consistency or workability), or the attainment of a higher slump at a given water content, or the use of less Portland cement to realize the same compressive strength. Superplasticizers, also called high range water reducing admixtures (HRWRs) belong to a new class of WRAs chemically different from the normal WRAs and capable of reducing water contents by about 30%, but a normal WRAs is capable of reducing water requirements by about 10%~15%.

2. Set accelerating admixtures

Set accelerating admixtures are best defined as those which, when added to concrete, mortar or paste, increase the rate of hydration of hydraulic cement, shorten the time of setting and increase the rate of early strength development. The class of admixtures is designated as Type C or Type E, and their performance requirements in Portland cement concrete are specified in ASTM C494.

66

3. Set retarding chemical admixtures

A set retarding admixture is defined as one that delays the time of setting of Portland cement paste and hence that of its mixtures, such as mortars and concrete. Consequences of this delay in the rate of hardening, or setting, include a delay in the development of the early strength of the concrete, mortar, or paste and an increase in later compress strength of the respective cementitious masses. There are three types of retarding admixtures recognized by ASTM: Type B, which simply retards the hydration of the Portland cement, Type D, which not only retards the hydration but also acts to disperse the cement and thereby provide water reduction, and finally Type G, which is a high range water reducing and set retarding admixture.

4. Air entraining admixtures

An air-entraining admixture is simply one that is added to either Portland cement paste, mortar, or concrete for the purpose of entraining air in the respective masses. Specification for materials proposed for use as air-entraining admixtures (AEAs) in concrete and the accepted method by which they are evaluated have been established by ASTM. While the earliest AEAs were animal tallow or complex hydrocarbons (oils/greases), which had been oxidized during the manufacture of cement and inadvertently found their way into concrete, the modern AEAs are more sophisticated in nature and are purposely added to concrete to produce the desired beneficial effects. Most of the modern AEAs are anionic in character because of the stability that they impart to the entrained air void. Cationic AEAs have been proposed foe use, but their cost is prohibitive and the stability that they provide to air void is questionable. A few nonionic materials, such as water-soluble low-molecular-weight ethylene oxide polymers, are being used, but they too offer very little stability to the entrained air void.

5. Pozzolan

The most often used mineral admixture in the modern concrete industry is the pozzolan, and there are many of them, is defined as siliceous or siliceous and aluminous materials which in themselves possess little or no cementitious value but will, in finely divided form and in the presence of moisture, chemically react which calcium hydroxide at ordinary temperatures to form compounds possessing cementitious properties. This chemical reaction between the siliceous and/or siliceous-alumina components in the pozzolan, calcium hydroxide and water is called the pozzolanic reaction. Two types of pozzolanic materials are readily available. They are the natural pozzolans and man-made pozzolans.

6. Other types admixtures

There are also some special types of admixtures. They include waterproofers, dispersing agents, etc. The most often used dispersing constituents of today's water-reducing admixtures and their supplementary components are listed in Table 5-1.

Table 5-1 components and their addition rates of modern water-reducing admixtures

Dispersant name	Addition rate*	Second ingredient	
		Name	Addition rate*
Alkali or earth metal salts of lingosulfonic acid	0.15	Triethanolamine calcium chloride	0.01 0.30
Carbohydrates, such as glucose and corn syrup	0.04	Triethanolamine calcium chloride	0.01 0.30
Alkali or alkaline earth metal salts of hydroxylated carboxylic acids(such as gluconic or heptogluconic acid)	0.06	Triethanolamine calcium chloride	0.01 0.30

Note:*-% solids on weight of cement.

New Words and Expressions

hydraulic	adj.	水硬性的，水力的
interground	vt.	相互研磨
dispersion	n.	分散，弥散
hydrocarbon	n.	烃碳氢化合物
dispersing agent		分散剂
inadvertently	adv.	疏忽地，不经意地
disperse	vt.	使分散，分配，传播
dispersant	n.	分散剂
grease	n.	油脂，润滑脂
anionic	adj.	阴离子的
dispersive	adj.	分散的，散开的，弥散的
cationic	adj.	阳离子的
alkali	n.	碱性，碱
alkali metal		碱金属
alkaline earth metals		碱土金属
prohibitive	adj.	抑制性的
non-ionic	adj.	非离子型的
soluble	adj.	可溶解的，可容的
ethylene	n.	乙烯
via	prep.	通过，经过，借助于
slump	n.	坍落度，滑动，塌陷度
polymer	n.	聚合物，聚合体
consistency	n.	稠度，一致性
siliceous	adj.	含硅的，硅酸的
workability	n.	可施工性，可塑性
aluminous	adj.	矾土的，含铝土的，铝酸的
mortar	n.	砂浆，灰浆泥
calcium lignosulfate		木质素磺酸钙
paste	n.	浆糊，浆料；vt. 用浆糊粘
lignosulfonic	adj.	木质素磺酸基的

68

tallow	n.	牛脂，动物脂，油脂
salicylic	adj.	水杨酸的
cementitious	adj.	有黏结性的，水泥质的
salicylic acid		水杨酸
superplasticizer	n.	高效塑化剂，超塑剂
steric hindrance		[化] 空间位阻，位阻（现象）
alumina	n.	氧化铝（亦称矾土）
aggressive	adj.	侵蚀性的
pozzolanic	adj.	凝硬性的，火山灰的
chloride	n.	氯化物
waterproofer	n.	防水层，防水剂，防水材料
nitrate	n.	硝酸盐
water-cement ratio		水灰比
nitrite	n.	亚硝酸盐
spatula	n.	刮勺，刮刀，刮铲
thiocyanate	n.	硫氰酸酯，硫氰酸盐
encapsulate	vt.	装入胶囊；vi. 形成胶囊
formate	n.	甲酸盐
finishing	ger.	修整，终饰，竣工
tirethanolamine	n.	三乙醇胺，三羟乙基胺
abutting	adj.	相邻的，接触的
untreated	adj.	未经处的，不处理的
agglomerate	n.	聚集，结块，团块
supplementary	adj.	补的，辅助的，附加的
entrap	vt.	诱捕，俘获，夹住
fluidity	n.	流动性，流度，液流性
postulate	n.	假说，假定，先决条件；vt. 假定，要求，以……为前提
adsorb	vt.	吸附；vi. 被吸附

Exercises

1. Translate the following sentences from English into Chinese.

(1) An admixture must not be confused with the term, addition, which is either inter-ground with or blended into a Portland cement during its manufacture.

(2) Water reducing chemical admixtures permits the use of less water to obtain the same slump(a measure of consistency or workability), or the attainment of a higher slump at given water content, or the use of less Portland content, or the use of less Portland cement to realize the same compressive strength.

(3) Set accelerating admixtures are best define as those which, when added to concrete, mortar or paste, increase the rate of hydration cement, shorten the time of setting and increase the rate of early strength development.

2. Translate the following sentences from Chinese into English.

(1) 外加剂被定义为除水、骨料和水泥外，在混凝土搅拌过程中掺入到其中的用量小、具有使混凝土增加某种特性（使用性能或工艺性能）作用的材料。

(2) 缓凝剂被定义为能够延缓波特兰水泥凝结时间，并因而延缓混凝土拌合料凝结时间的材料。

(3) 在现代混凝土业中最常用的矿物掺合料是火山灰。

Unit 6 about High Performance Construction Materials

Since the 1980's, the design and construction use more and more high performance materials. High performance construction materials provide far greater strength, ductility, durability, and resistance to external elements than traditional construction materials, and can significantly increase the longevity of structures in the built environment and can also reduce maintenance costs for these structures considerably. These most significant high performance construction materials include high performance concrete, high performance steel, fiber reinforced cement composites, FRP composites, etc.

The United States, the Strategic Highway Research Programe (SHRP) sponsored a project on High Performance Concrete in 1987. In an effort to improve and extend the service life of bridges, the Federal Highway Administration (FHWA) initiated a national program in 1993 to implement high-performance concrete (HPC) in bridges. Fiber reinforced cement composites and FRP composites are becoming more and more popular because their unique mechanical properties and corrosion resistance.

The other trend is the combined use of several different types of high performance materials in one structure. The combination or composite structures made of several high performance materials could maximize the advantages of these components. High strength steels and high strength concretes have been tested or used in composite construction. It has been found that in addition to strength and serviceability, stability, local buckling and ductility are also important effects in the design of composite members incorporating high strength materials.

In addition to these technical advantages, the use of high performance materials can have very significant economic advantages as well. The materials cost of high performance materials is usually higher than conventional materials due to the special requirements for raw materials and manufacturing processes. However, these materials maybe only one component in construction, and the total cost of the finished construction is more important than the cost of an individual material. According to a study by Moreno, the use of 41MPa compressive strength concrete in the lower columns of a 23-story commercial building requires a 865mm square column at a cost of $9.90/m^2. The use of 83MPa concrete allows a reduction in column size to 610 mm square at a cost of $5.60/m^2. In addition to the reduction in initial cost, a smaller column size results in less intrusion in the lower stories of commercial space and, thereby, more rentable floor space.

In addition to increasing the duration of structures, high performance materials are also valuable because they can improve the efficiency of design and construction practices. For instance, sustainable design and construction, an innovative building approach that incorporates high standards of environmental protection with an emphasis on life-cycle cost considerations, often uses high performance materials because these substances are more environmentally friendly and possess greater recyclable capability than conventional construction materials. The use of high performance materials to increase service life of a structure from 50 years to 100 years will save far more than the amount of money for the original construction cost of the structure. Also, it will conserve natural resources and reduce negative impacts on the environment. Moreover, many of these materials are often much easier and faster to install than conventional construction materials, a key advantage for the many fast-track projects delivered using design-build.

More and more people have been harnessing the advancement in smart materials technology for structural engineering applications. Specifically, the use of smart sensors and actuators as well as advanced signal processing and computational techniques are explored and adapted for structural health monitoring and control of structures. One good example is the Confederation Bridge, which was completed in 1997 and connects the Provinces of Prince Edward Island (PEI) and New Brunswick (NB) on the east coast of Canada. The 12.9km long Confederation Bridge is the world's longest prestressed concrete box girder bridge built over salt water. With 45 main spans of 250m each and a 100-year design life, the design criteria of the Confederation Bridge are not covered by any code or standard in the world. With a design life of 100 years, the use of high performance concrete and careful attention to production and construction practices were imperative. Over 400000 cubic meters of concrete was used for the structure. The proposed high-performance concretes were extensively tested for durability, especially through freeze-thaw cycles, sulfate resistivity and chloride diffusivity testing, checking of alkali content and alkali/aggregate reactivity, evaluation of curing regimes for the huge components, etc. Precasting was chosen for improved quality, as well as reduced construction time. A comprehensive monitoring and research program is being carried out to monitor and study the behavior and performance of the bridge under ice forces, short-and long-term deformations, thermal stresses, traffic load and load combinations, dynamic response due to wind and earthquake, and corrosion, and to obtain critical information that engineers now lack in these areas .

New Words and Expressions

ductility	n.	韧性
durability	n.	耐久性
longevity	n.	寿命
maintenance cost		维修费用
sponsor	v.	发起
component	n.	组分

harness	v.	利用
innovative	adj.	革新的
chloride	n.	氯化物
diffusivity	n.	扩散

Exercises

1. Translate the following sentences from English into Chinese.

(1) The other trend is the combined use of several different types of high performance materials in one structure.

(2) The use of high performance materials to increase service life of a structure from 50 years to 100 years will save far more than the amount of money for the original construction cost of the structure.

2. Translate the following sentences from Chinese into English.

(1) 除了可以增加建筑物的寿命外, 高性能材料还可以提高建筑物的使用率。

(2)（如果）高性能材料的使用可以将建筑物的服务年限延长 50～100 年, 则它可以节约比建筑物本身造价还要多的费用。

Unit 7　Prestressed Concrete

Concrete is strong in compression, but weak in tensions: its tensile strength varies from 8 to 14 percent of its compressive strength. Due to such a low tensile capacity, flexural cracks develop at early stages of loading. In order to reduce or prevent such cracks from developing, a concentric or eccentric force is imposed in the longitudinal direction of the structural element. This force prevents the cracks from developing by eliminating or considerably reducing the tensile stress at the critical midspan and support sections at service load, thereby raising the bending, shear, and torsional capacities of the sections[①]. The sections are then able to behave elastically, and almost the full capacity of the concrete in compression can be efficiently utilized across the entire depth of the concrete sections when all loads act on the structure.

Such an imposed longitudinal force is called a prestressed force, i.e., a compressive force that prestresses the sections along the span of the structural element prior to the application of the transverse gravity dead and live loads or transient horizontal live loads. The type of presressing force involved, together with its magnitude, are determined mainly on the basis of the type of system to be constructed and the span length and slenderness desired. Since the prestressing force is applied longitudinally along or parallel to axis of the member, the prestressing principle involved is commonly known as linear prestressing.

Circular prestressing, used in liquid containment tanks, pipes, and pressure reactor vessels, essentially follows the same basic principles, as does linear prestressing. The circumferential hoop, or "hugging" stress on the cylindrical or spherical structure, neutralizes the tensile stresses at the outer fibers of the curvilinear surface caused by the internal contained pressure.

From the preceding discussion, it is plain that permanent stresses in the prestressed structural member are created before the full dead and live loads are applied in order to eliminate or considerably reduce the net tensile stresses caused by these loads. With reinforced concrete, it is assumed that the tensile strength of the concrete is negligible and disregarded. This is because the tensile forces resulting from the bending moments are resisted by the bond created in the reinforcement process. Cracking and deflection are therefore essentially irrecoverable in reinforced concrete once the member has reached its limit state at service load.

The reinforcement in the reinforced concrete member does not exert any force of its own on the member, contrary to the action of prestressing steel. The steel required to produce the prestressing force in the prestressed member actively preloads the member, permitting a relatively high controlled recovery of cracking and deflection. Once the flexural tensile strength of the concrete is exceeded, the prestressed member starts to act like a reinforced concrete element.

Prestressed member are shallower in depth than their reinforced concrete counterparts for the same span and loading conditions. In general, the depth of a prestressed concrete member is

73

usually about 65 to 80 percent of the depth of the equivalent reinforced concrete member. Hence, the prestressed member requires less concrete, and about 20 to 35 percent of the amount of reinforcement. Unfortunately, this saving in material weight is balanced by the higher cost of the higher quality materials needed in prestressing. Also, regardless of the system used, prestressing operations themselves result in an added cost: formwork is more complex, since the geometry of prestressed sections is usually composed of flanged sections with thin webs.

In spite of these additional costs, if a large enough number of precast units are manufactured, the difference between at least the initial costs of prestressed and reinforced concrete systems is usually not very large. And the indirect long-term savings are quite substantial, because less maintenance is needed, a longer working life is possible due to better quality control of the concrete, and lighter foundations are achieved due to the smaller cumulative weight of the superstructure.

Once the beam span of reinforced concrete exceeds 70 to 90 feet (21.3 to 27.4m), the dead weight of the beam becomes excessive, resulting in heavier members and, consequently, greater long-term deflection and cracking. Thus, for larger spans, prestressed concrete becomes mandatory since arches are expensive to construct and do not perform as well due to the severe long-term shrinkage and creep they undergo. Very large spans such as segmental bridges or cable-stayed bridges can only be constructed through the use of prestressing.

Prestressed concrete is not a new concept, dating back to 1872, when P.H. Jackson, an engineer from California, patented a prestressing system that used a tie rod to construct beams or arches from individual blocks. After a long lapse of time during which little progress was made because of the unavailability of high-strength steel to overcome prestress losses, R.E. Dill of Alexandria, Nenraska, recognized the effect of the shrinkage and creep (transverse material flow) of concrete on the loss of prestress. He subsequently developed the idea that successive post-tensioning of unbonded rods would compensate for the time-dependent loss of stress in the rods due to the decrease in the length of the member because of creep and shrinkage. In the early 1920s, W. H. Hewett of Minneapolis developed the principles of circular prestressing. He hoop-stressed horizontal reinforcement around walls of concrete tanks through the use of turnbuckles to prevent cracking due to internal liquid pressure, thereby achieving watertightness. Thereafter, prestressing of tanks and pipes developed at an accelerated pace in the United States, with thousands of tanks for water, liquid, and gas storage built and much mileage of prestressed pressure pipe laid in the two to three decades that followed.

Linear prestressing had progressed a long way from the early days, in particular through the ingenuity of Eugene Freyssinet, who proposed in 1926-28 methods to overcome prestress losses through the use of high-strength and high–ductility steels. In 1940, he introduced the now well-known and well-accepted Freyssinet system[②].

P. W. Abeles of England introduced and developed the concept of partial ptestressing between the 1930s and 1960s. F. Leonhardt of Germany, V. Mikhailov of Russia, and T.Y. Lin of the United States also contributed a great deal to the art and science of the design of

74

prestressed concrete. Lin's load-balancing method deserves particular mention in this regard, as it considerably simplified the design process, particularly in continuous structures. These twentieth-century developments have led to the extensive use of prestressing throughout the world, and in the United States in particular.

Today, prestressed concrete is used in buildings, underground structures, TV towers, floating storage and offshore structures, power stations, nuclear reactor vessels, and numerous types of bridge systems including segmental and cable-stayed bridges, they demonstrate the versatility of the prestressing concept and its all-encompassing application. The success in the development and construction of all these structures has been due in no small measures to the advances in the technology of materials, particularly prestressing steel, and the accumulated knowledge in estimating the short-and long-term losses in the prestressing forces.

New Words and Expressions

longitudinal	*a.*	纵向的
transverse	*a.*	横向的
transient	*a., n.*	瞬间，瞬态
slenderness	*n.*	细长（度）
circumferential	*a.*	周围的，环形的，环绕的
hoop	*n.,v.*	箍筋；箍住
spherical	*a.*	球（形）的
irrecoverable	*a.*	不能恢复的
formwork	*n.*	模板，支模
flange	*n.*	（梁的）翼缘
web	*n.*	（梁的）腹板
superstructure	*n.*	上部结构
mandatory	*a.*	必须遵循的，命令的
turnbuckle	*n.*	松紧螺旋扣
ingenuity	*n.*	独创性，机灵
flexural crack		挠曲裂缝
critical section		临界截面
service (live, dead) load		使用（活，静）荷载
prestressing force		预应力
precast unit		预制构件
time-dependent		与时间有关的，时变
partial prestressing		部分预应力
cable-stayed bridge		斜拉桥

Notes

① thereby 与现在分词 raising…连用一般表示结果。
② Freyssinet system 弗莱西奈式（预应力）体系，简称弗氏体系

Exercises

1. Translate the following sentences from English into Chinese.

(1) This force prevents the cracks from developing by eliminating or considerably reducing the tensile stresses at the critical midspan and support sections at service load, thereby raising the bending shear, and torsional capacities of the sections.

(2) The success in the development and construction of all these structures has been due in no small measures to the advances in the technology of materials, particularly prestressing steel, and accumulated knowledge in estimating the short- and long-term losses in the prestressing forces.

2. Translate the following sentences from Chinese into English.

(1) 混凝土的长期收缩和徐变对预应力损失产生很大影响。

(2) 必须采用高强度、高延性钢作为预加应力的材料。

Unit 8 Principles of Polymer Modification for Cement Composites

Polymer-modified mortar and concrete are prepared by mixing either a polymer or monomer in a dispersed, powdery, or liquid form with fresh cement mortar and concrete mixtures, and subsequently curing, and if necessary, the monomer contained in the mortar or concrete is polymerized in situ.

Several types of polymer-modified mortars and concretes, i.e., latex-redispersible polymer powder-, water-soluble polymer-, liquid resin-, and monomer-modified mortars and concretes, are produced by using the polymers and monomers. Of these, the latex-modified mortar and concrete are by far the most widely used cement modifiers.

Although polymers and monomers in any form such as latexes, water-soluble polymers, liquid resins, and monomets are used in cement composites such as mortar and concrete, it is very important that both cement hydration and polymer phase formation (coalescence of polymer particles and the polymerization of monomers) proceed well to yield a monolithic matrix phase with a network structure in which the hydrated cement phase and polymer phase interpenetrate[①]. In the polymer-modified mortar and concrete structures, aggregates are bound by such a co-matrix phase, resulting in the superior properties of polymer-modified mortar and concrete compared to conventional.

1 Principles of Latex Modification

Latex modification of cement mortar and concrete is governed by both cement hydration and polymer film formation processes in their binder phase. The cement hydration process generally precedes the polymer. In due course, a co-matrix phase is formed by both formation process cement hydration and polymer film formation processes. It is important to understand the mechanism of the co-matrix phase formation.

Mechanism of Polymer-Cement and Co-matrix Formation.

It is believed that a co-matrix phase which consists of cement gel and polymer films is generally formed as a binder according to a three-step simplified model. Grosskurth proposed a similar model indicating the formation of the polymer-cement co-matrix. Sugita, et al have recently investigated the microstructures and composite mechanism of latex-modified pastes and mortars, and found the interfacial layer of cement hydrates with a large amount of polymer particles on the aggregates and cement particles. As a result, both the particle dispersion of the polymer and the formation of polymer films are necessary for explaining the composite mechanism of the latex-modified systems.

77

The process of the polymer film formation on the cement hydrates is represented in following paragraph

First Step. When polymer latexes are mixed with fresh cement mortar or concrete, the polymer particles are uniformly dispersed in the cement paste phase. In this polymer-cement paste, the cement gel is gradually formed by the cement hydration and the water phase is saturated with calcium hydroxide formed during the hydration, whereas the polymer particles deposit partially on the surfaces of the cement-gel-unhydrated-cement particle mixtures. It is likely that the calcium hydroxide in the water phase reacts with a silica surface of the aggregates to form a calcium silicate layer. It is confirmed that the formation of the calcium hydroxide and ettringite in the contact zone between the cement hydrates and aggregates is attributed to the bond between them.

Su, Bijen and Larbi found from studies on the interaction between latex-modified pastes and aggregates that calcium hydroxide [$Ca(OH)_2$] crystals are formed at the contact zone or interfacial zone between the cement hydrates and limestone or granite in the presence of the polymer latexes and oriented with their c-axes perpendicular to the interface.

Afridi etal pointed out that the behavior and morphology of calcium hydroxide crystals formed in latex-modified mortars affect their properties.

Second Step, With drainage due to the development of the cement gel structure, the polymer particles are gradually confined in the capillary pores. As the cement hydration proceeds further and the capillary water is reduced, the polymer particles flocculate to form a continuous close-packed layer of polymer particles on the surfaces of the cement-gel-unhydrated-cement particle mixtures and simultaneously adhere to the mixtures and the silicate layer over the aggregate surfaces. In this case, the larger pores in the mixtures are found to be filled by the adhesive and autohesive polymer particles. This may be explained by considering that the size of the pores in the cement paste ranges from a few hundred picometers to several hundred nanometers, whereas that of the polymer particles in a typical latex ranges from 50 to 500 nanometers.Some chemical reactions may take place between the particle surfaces of reactive polymers such as polyacrylic esters (PAE), poly(s tyrene-acrylic ester) (SAE), poly(vinylidene chloride-vinyl chloride) (PVDC) and chloroprene rubber (CR) latexes and calcium ions (Ca^{2+}), calcium hydroxide [$Ca(OH)_2$] crystal surfaces, or silicate surfaces over the aggregates. the effects of the chemical bonds on the properties of the latex-modified mortars and concretes appear to be governed by their volume fraction in the latex-modified mortars and concretes, and the chemical bonds do not necessarily act effectively to improve the properties. The effects of the chemical bonds are apt to be offset by increasing entraining air as discussed later.

Third Step. Ultimately, with water withdrawal by cement hydration, the close-packed polymer particles on the cement hydrates coalesce into continuous films or membranes, and the films or membranes bind the cement hydrates together to form a monolithic network in which the polymer phase interpenetrates throughout the cement hydrate phase. Such a structure acts as a matrix phase for latex-modified mortar and concrete, and the aggregates are bound by the matrix phase to the hardened mortar and concrete.

The pore structure of latex-modified systems is influenced by the type of polymer in the latexes used and polymer-cement ratio as discussed in detail later. The total porosity or pore volume generally tends to decrease with an increase in the polymer-cement ratio. This contributes to improve cements in the impermeability, resistance to carbonation, and freeze-thaw durability.

2　Modification with Redispersible Polymer Powders

The principle of modification of cement mortar and concrete with redispersible polymer powders is almost the same as that of latex modification except that it involves the addition of redispersible polymer powders. Mostly the redispersible polymer powders are used by dry mixing with the cement and aggregate premixtures, followed by wet mixing them with water. During the wet mixing, the redispersible polymer powders are reemulsified in the modified mortar and concrete, and behave in the same manner as the latexes for cement modifiers.

3　Modification with Water-Soluble Polymers

In the modification with water-soluble polymers such as cellulose derivatives and polyvinyl alcohol, small amounts of the polymers are added as powders or aqueous solutions to cement mortar and concrete during mixing. Such a modification mainly improves their workability because of the surface activity of the water-soluble polymers, and prevents the "dry-out" phenomena). The prevention of the "dry-out" is interpreted in terms of an increase in the viscosity of the water phase in the modified cement mortar and concrete and a sealing effect due to the formation of very thin and water-impervious film in them. In general, the water-soluble polymers hardly contribute to an improvement in the strength of the modified systems.

4　Modification with Liquid Resins

In the modification with liquid thermosetting resins, considerable amounts of polymerisable low-molecular weight polymers or prepolymers are added in a liquid form to cement mortar and concrete during mixing. The polymer content of the modified mortar and concrete generally is higher than that of latex-modified systems. In this modification, polymerization is initiated in the presence of water to form a polymer phase, and simultaneously the cement hydration occurs. As a result, a co-matrix phase is formed with a network structure of interpenetrating polymer and cement hydrate phases, and this binds aggregates strongly. Consequently, the strength and other properties of the modified mortar and concrete are improved in much the same way as those of the latex-modified systems.

5 Modification with Monomers

The principle of modification of cement composites with monomers is about the same as that of liquid resin modification except that it involves the addition of monomers instead of the liquid resins. In such a modification, considerable quantities of the monomers are mixed with the cement mortar and concrete, and both polymerization and cement hydration occur at the same time, during or after curing, to make a monolithic matrix which binds aggregates. Generally, such a modification has not been successful because of the poor properties of the modified systems. The reasons for this are the interference with the cement hydration, the degradation of the monomers by the alkalis from the cement and the difficulty in uniformly dispersing the monomers and other components during mixing.

New Words and Expressions

polymer	n.	聚合物
monomer	n.	单体
polymerize	v.	使聚合
situ	n.	原位
latex	n.	胶乳
soluble	adj.	可溶解的
resin	n.	合成树脂
coalescence	n.	聚合
particle	n.	颗粒
monolithic	adj.	整体的
calcium hydroxide		氢氧化钙
ettringite	n.	钙矾石
limestone	n.	石灰石
granite	n.	花岗岩
morphology	n.	形态
flocculate	v.	絮凝
nanometer	n.	纳米
polyacrylic	n.	聚丙烯
chloroprene	n.	氯丁二烯
membrane	n.	膜
premixtures	n.	预混合物
cellulose	n.	纤维
derivative	n.	衍生物
polyvinyl alcohol		聚乙烯醇

Notes

① Although …, it is very important that …with a network structure in which….

本句中，although 引导让步状语从句，主句为 it is…，在主句中，it 为形式主语，真正的主语为 that 从句，with 短语作伴随状语，which 引导定语从句，其先行语为 structure。

Exercises

1. Translate the following sentences from English into Chinese.

(1) When polymer latexes are mixed with fresh cement mortar or concrete, the polymer particles are uniformly dispersed in the cement paste phase.

(2) The principle of modification of cement composites with monomers is about the same as that of liquid resin modification except that it involves the addition of monomers instead of the liquid resins.

2. Translate the following sentences from Chinese into English.

(1) 聚合物改性混凝土有许多与普通混凝土不一样的性能。

(2) 聚合物混凝土的反应不仅有水泥的水化，还有聚合物的反应。

Unit 9　Smart Material

Whether a structural material is load bearing or not in a structure, its strength and stiffness are important[①]. Although purely structural applications dominate, combined structural and nonstructural applications are increasingly important as smart structures and electronics become more common. Such combined applications are facilitated by smart materials, which include multifunctional structural materials and non-structural functional materials . The functions include sensing, which is relevant to smart structures, structural vibration control, traffic monitoring and structural health monitoring[②]. They also include damping, thermal insulation, electrical grounding, resistance heating (say, for deicing), controlled electrical conduction, electromagnetic interference shielding, lateral guidance of vehicles, thermoelectricity, piezoresistivity, etc.

In addition to mechanical properties, a structural material may be required to have other properties, such as low density (light weight) for fuel saving in the case of aircraft and automobiles, for high speed in the case of race bicycles, and for handleability in the case of wheelchairs and armor. Another property that is often required is corrosion resistance, which is desirable for the durability of all structures, particularly automobiles and bridges. Yet another property that may be required is the ability to withstand high temperatures and/or thermal cycling as heat may be encountered by the structure during operation, maintenance or repair.

A relatively new trend is for a structural material to be able to serve functions other than the structural function, so that the material becomes multifunctional (a kin to killing two or more birds with one stone, thereby saving cost and simplifying design). An example of a non-structural function is the sensing of damage. Such sensing, also called structural health monitoring, is valuable for the prevention of hazards. It is particularly important to aging aircraft and bridges[③]. The sensing function can be attained by embedding sensors (such as optical fibers, the damage or strain of which affects the light throughput) in the structure. However, the embedding usually causes degradation of the mechanical properties and the embedded devices are costly and poor in durability compared to the structural material. Another way to attain the sensing function is to detect the change in property (e.g., the electrical resistivity) of the structural material due to damage. In this way, the structural material serves as its own sensor and is said to be self-sensing. Such multifunctional structural materials are also referred to as intrinsically smart materials. Intrinsic smartness is to be distinguished from extrinsic smartness, which relies on embedded or attached devices rather than the structural materials themselves in order to attain a certain non-structural function.

Self-Actuating Materials

Self-actuating materials refer to structural materials that provide strain or stress in response to an input such as an electric field or a magnetic field. In the case of an electric field, the phenomenon pertains to either the reverse piezoelectric effect or electrostriction. In the case of a magnetic field, the phenomenon pertains to magnetostriction.

Sensing allows a structure to know its situation, whereas actuation is a way of allowing a structure to respond to what has been sensed. Thus, the presence of both self-sensing and self-actuating abilities enables a structural material to be really smart.

Self-actuating structural materials have not yet been well developed, although there are reports of self-actuation in the form of the reverse piezoelectric effect in carbon fiber (short) cement and in carbon fiber (continuous) polymer-matrix composite.

Self-Healing Material

Self-healing refers to the ability of a structural material to heal or repair itself automatically upon the sensing of damage. This ability enhances safety, which is particularly needed for strategic structures. A self-healing cement-based material that involves the embedment of macroscopic tubules of an adhesive in selected locations of the cement- based material has been reported. The tubule fractures upon damage of the structural material, thereby allowing the adhesive to ooze out of the tubule. The adhesive fills the crack in its vicinity, thus causing healing. This technology suffers from the structural degradation due to the embedment of the tubules and the inability of a given tubule location to provide healing after the first time of damage infliction. Once the tubule has broken and the adhesive has solidified, the tubule cannot provide the healing function any more.

The problem with tubules may be circumvented by using a microencapsulated monomer, i.e., microcapsules containing a monomer. Upon breaking of the microcapsule, the monomer oozes out and meets the catalyst that is present in the structural material outside the microcapsule. Reaction between the monomer and the catalyst causes the formation of a polymer, which fills the crack. This method of self-healing has been shown to a limited extent in polymers, but not in cement-based materials, due to the pores in cement-based materials acting as sinks for the polymer. Furthermore, the microcapsule method suffers from the high cost of the catalyst, which needs to be able to promote polymerization at room temperature (without heating). It also suffers from the toxicity of the monomer.

New Words and Expressions

smart	adj.	智能的
stiffness	n.	刚度，抗挠性
multifunctional	adj.	多功能的
thermal	adj.	热的
insulation	n.	绝缘
electromagnetic	adj.	电磁的
thermoelectricity	n.	热电
piezoresistivity	n.	压电电阻效应

mechanical	adj.	机械的
density	n.	密度
handleability	n.	可操作性
withstand	v.	承受
encounter	v.	遭受
hazard	n.	危害
embed	v.	把……牢牢地嵌入（或插入、埋入）
optical	adj.	光学的
intrinsically	adv.	从本质上讲
ooze	v.	使(液体)缓缓流出
polymerization	n.	聚合
toxicity	n.	毒性
monomer	n.	单体

Notes

① …, its strength …

这是一个让步状语从句。全句可分成两句：不管结构材料在结构中受力与否，其强度和刚度是非常重要的性能。

② … ,which is…

这是一个定语从句，which 引导的定语从句修饰 sensing，which 后面全部为定语从句。

③ It is…

句中的 it 是形式主语，真实主语是不定式 to aging aircraft and bridges。

Exercises

1. Translate the following sentences from English into Chinese.

(1) Whether a structural material is load bearing or not in a structure, its strength and stiffness are important.

(2) In addition to mechanical properties, a structural material may be required to have other properties, such as low density (light weight) for fuel saving in the case of aircraft and automobiles, for high speed in the case of race bicycles, and for handle ability in the case of wheelchairs and armor.

(3) A relatively new trend is for a structural material to be able to serve functions other than the structural function, so that the material becomes multifunctional (a kin to killing two or more birds with one stone, thereby saving cost and simplifying design).

2. Translate the following sentences from Chinese into English.

(1) 由于材料的绝热性与材料密度成反比，因而轻质混凝土的绝热性比普通混凝土好。

(2) 自修复指的是材料在受到损害后可以对其本身自动地进行修复的能力。

84

Unit 10 Modern Buildings and Structural Materials

Many great buildings built in earlier ages are still in existence and in use. Among them are the Pantheon and Colosseum in Rome, Hagia Sophia in Istanbul; the Gothic churches of France and England, and the Renaissance cathedrals, with their great domes, like the Duomo in Florence and St. Peter's in Rome[①]. They are massive structures with thick stone walls that counteract the thrust of their great weight. Thrust is the pressure exerted by each part of a structure on its other parts.

These great buildings were not the product of knowledge of mathematics and physics. They were constructed instead on the basis of experience and observation, often as the result of trial and error. One of the reasons they have survived is because of the great strength that was built into them-strength greater than necessary in most cases[②]. But the engineers of earlier times also had their failure. In Rome, for example, most of the people lived in insular, great tenement blocks that were often ten stories high. Many of them were poorly constructed and sometimes collapsed with considerable loss of life.

Today, however, the engineer has the advantage not only of empirical information, but also of scientific data that permit him to make careful calculations in advance. When a modern engineer plans a structure, he takes into account the total weight of all its component materials. This is known as the dead load, which is the weight of the structure itself. He must also consider the live load, the weight of all the people, cars, furniture, machines, and so on that the structure will support when it is in use. In structures such as bridges that will handle fast automobile traffic, he must consider the impact, the force at which the live load will be exerted on the structure. He must also determine the safety factor, that is, an additional capability to make the structure stronger than the combination of the three other factors.

The modern engineer must also understand the different stresses to which the materials in a structure are subject. These include the opposite forces of compression and tension. In compression the material is pressed or pushed together; in tension the material is pulled apart or stretched, like a rubber band. In addition to tension and compression, another force is at work, namely shear, which we defined as the tendency of a material to fracture along the lines of stress. The shear might occur in a vertical plane, but it also might run along the horizontal axis of the beam, the neutral plane, where there is neither tension nor compression.

Altogether, three forces can act on a structure: vertical-those that act up or down; horizontal-those that act sideways; and those that act upon it with a rotating or turning motion. Forces that act at an angle are a combination of horizontal and vertical forces. Since the structures designed by civil engineers are intended to be stationary or stable, these forces must be kept in balance. The vertical forces, for example, must be equal to each other. If a beam supports a load above, the beam itself must have sufficient strength to counterbalance that weight. The horizontal forces must also equal each other so that there is not too much thrust either to the right or to the left. And forces that might pull the structure around must he countered with forces that pull in the opposite direction.

One of the most spectacular engineering failures of modern tines, the collapse of the Tacoma Narrows Bridge in 1940, was the result of not considering the last of these factors carefully enough. When strong gusts of wind, up to sixty-five kilometers an hour, struck the bridge during a storm, they set up waves along the roadway of the bridge and also a lateral motion that caused the roadway to fall. Fortunately, engineers learn from mistakes, so it is now common practice to test scale models of bridges in wind runnels for aerodynamic resistance.

The principal construction materials of earlier tines were wood and masonry brick, stone, or tile, and similar materials. The courses or layers were bound together with mortar or bitumen, a tar-like substance, or some other binding agent. The Greeks and Romans sometimes used iron rods or clamps to strengthen their buildings. The columns of the Parthemon in Athens, for example, have holes drilled in them for iron bars that have now rusted away[3]. The Romans also used a natural cement called pozzolana, made from volcanic ash, that became as hard as stone under water.

Both steel and cement, the two most important construction materials of modern times, were introduced in the nineteenth century. Steel, basically an alloy of iron and a small amount of carbon, had been made up to that tine by a laborious process that restricted it to such special uses as sword blades. After the invention of the Bessemer process[4] in 1856, steel was available in large quantities at low prices. The enormous advantage of steel is its tensile strength; that is, it does not lose its strength when it is under a calculated degree of tension, a force which, as we have seen, tends to pull apart many materials[5]. New alloys have further increased the strength of steel and eliminated some of its problems, such as fatigue, which is a tendency for it to weaken as a result of continual changes in stress.

Modern cement, called Portland cement, was invented in 1824. It is a mixture of limestone and clay, which is heated and then ground into a powder. It is mixed at or near the construction site with sand, aggregate (small stones, crushed rock, or gravel), and water to make concrete. Different proportions of the ingredients produce concrete with different strength and weight. Concrete is very versatile; it can be poured, pumped, or even sprayed into all kinds of shapes. And whereas steel has great tensile strength, concrete has great strength under compression. Thus, the two substances complement each other.

They also complement each other in another way: they have almost the same rate of contraction and expansion. They therefore can work together in situations where both compression and tension are factors. Steel rods are embedded in concrete to make reinforced concrete in concrete beams or structures where tension will develop. Concrete and steel also form such a strong bond-the force that unites them-that the steel cannot slip within the concrete. Still another advantage is that steel does not rust in concrete. Acid corrodes steel, whereas concrete has an alkaline chemical reaction, the opposite if acid.

Prestressed concrete is an improved form of reinforcement. Steel rods are bent into the shapes to give them the necessary degree of tensile strength. They are then used to prestress concrete, usually by pretensioning or posttensioning method. Prestressed concrete has made it possible to develop buildings with unusual shapes, like some of the modern sports arenas, with large spaces unbroken by any obstructing supports⑥. The uses for this relatively new structural method are constantly being developed.

The current tendency is to develop lighter materials. Aluminum, for example, weighs much less than steel but has many of the same properties. Aluminum beams have already been uses for bridge construction and for the framework of a few buildings.

Attempts are also being made to produce concrete with more strength and durability, and with a lighter weight. One system that helps cut concrete weight to some extent uses polymers, which are long chainlike compounds used in plastics, as part of the mixture⑦.

New Words and Expressions

counteract	v.	抵抗，平衡
insula	n.	群房、公寓
thrust	n.,v.	推，推力
tenement	n.	出租的房子，经济公寓
concave	adj.,n.	凹的，凹面
convex	adj.,n.	凸的，凸面
shear	n.,v.	剪切，剪力
roadway	n.	车行道，路面
masonry	n.	亏工，砌筑
mortar	n.	砂浆，灰浆
bitumen	n.	沥青
tar-like	adj.	焦油般的
clamp	n.,v.	夹子，夹钳；卡紧
cement	n.	水泥
aggregate	n.	骨料，集料
ingredient	n.	（混合物）成分，配料
versatile	adj.	多用途的，多方面适应的
alkaline	adj.	碱性（的）
arena	n.	表演场
polymer	n.	聚合物
fatigue	n.	疲劳
trail and error		反复试验，试错法，尝试法
dead load		恒载
live load		活载
volcanic ash		火山灰

safety factor	安全系数
neutral plane	中性面
rotating or turning moment	旋转力矩，扭转力矩
wind tunnel(test)	风洞（试验）
tensile strength	抗拉强度
binding agent	黏结料，结合料，粘合剂
volcanic ash	火山灰
Portland cement	波特兰水泥，硅酸盐水泥
construction site	施工现场
reinforced concrete	钢筋混凝土
prestressed concrete	预应力混凝土
pretensioning(posttensing) concrete	先（后）张法

Notes

① Pantheon 潘提翁神庙（公元前 120～124 年），位于意大利罗马；Colosseum 罗马大斗兽场（78～80 年）；Hagia Sophia 圣索非亚教堂（533～537 年），位于土耳其伊斯坦布尔；Duomo （意大利语），意为 cathedral；St. Peter's 指罗马圣彼得大教堂（1506～1626 年），当时是在拉斐尔和米开朗琪罗等伟大艺术家们的亲自指导下建立起来的，是文艺复兴建筑中最完美的代表。

② 比较级 + than (it is)necessary 超过了所需要的……此处省略了。Strength greater than necessary in most cases 是破折号前面 great strength 的同位语。

③ Parthenon 帕提侬神庙，指古希腊雅典城邦的保护神雅典娜·帕提侬的神庙，是古希腊全盛时期建筑与雕刻的主要代表作。

④ Bessemer process 贝色麦法，又称酸性底吹转炉炼钢法，由英国冶金学家 Henry Bessemer 在 1856 年首创。这是一种不需外热的、可大量生产的炼钢方法。

⑤ a force which, as we have seen, tends to … 这是 a calculated degree of tension（特定程度的拉力）的同位语，as we have seen 是定语从句中的插入语。译为：就像我们已经知道的那种能把多种材料拉断的力。

⑥ with large spaces unbroken by… 这个介词短语作状语用。译为：它们的大空间没有任何挡住视线的支撑物。

⑦ One system that helps cut concrete weight to some extent uses polymers, which are long chainlike compounds used in plastics, as part of the mixture.
有一种用聚合物（塑料中用的长链化合物）作为部分配料的方法，这种方法有助于使混凝土的重量降到一定程度。

Exercises

1. Translate the following sentences from English into Chinese.

(1) In addition to tension and compression, another force is at work, namely shear, which we defined as the tendency of a material to fracture along the lines of stress.

(2) The enormous advantage of steel is its tensile strength; that is, it does not lose its strength when it is under a calculated degree of tension, a force which, as we have seen, tends to pull apart many materials.

2. Translate the following sentences from Chinese into English.

(1) 目前，正在试图（attempt）生产出强度更高、耐久性更好且重量更轻的混凝土。

(2) 一般，材料承受（subject）拉力，或压力，或剪力，或这些力的组合作用。

Unit 11   Ceramic Fabrication Process: Conventional Routes to Ceramics

Solid ceramic bodies are generally produced by using the process of powder compaction followed by firing at high temperature. Sintering or densification occurs during this heat treatment and is associated with joining together of particles, volume reduction, decrease in porosity and increase in grain size. The phase distribution or microstructure within the ceramic is developed during sintering and fabrication techniques used for shaping ceramics are described here. The aim of these techniques is to produce microstructures suitable for particular applications.

Precipitation from Solution

Alumina occurs as the mineral bauxite and is refined in the Bayer process whereby ore is initially dissolved under pressure in sodium hydroxide so that solid impurities (SiO_2, TiO_2, Fe_2O_3) separate from sodium aluminate solution. This solution is either seeded with gibbsite crystals (α-$Al_2O_3 \cdot 3H_2O$) or undergoes autoprecipitation to bayerite (β-$Al_2O_3 \cdot 3H_2O$) after its neutralization with CO_2 gas. Temperature, alumina supersaturation and amount of seed affect particle size during crystallization.

Problems can arise when two or more components are coprecipitated. Thus, different species do not always deposit from solution at the reaction PH, while washing procedures can selectively remove a precipitated component as well as dissolve entrained electrolyte. The difficulty in maintaining chemical homogeneity is serious as inhomogeneities has a deleterious effect on the mechanical and electrical properties of ceramics. Because precipitation results in agglomerated powders, grinding, dry-milling or wet-milling with water or a non-aqueous liquid are used for particle size reduction so that powder compacts will sinter to near theoretical density[①].

Precipitation reactions are not restricted to oxides and hydroxides. Hence, for the high T_c oxide superconductor $La_{1.85}Ba_{0.15}CuO_4$, La, Ba and Cu oxalates were deposited from electrolyte solutions and sintered in air at 1373 K. because these materials reversibly intercalate O_2, the annealing temperature and rate of cooling, which affect their superconducting properties and the Cu^{3+}/Cu^{2+} ratio must be carefully controlled.

Powder Mixing Techniques

Multicomponent oxide powders are synthesized from conventional mixing techniques by initially blending together starting materials, usually metal oxides and carbonates, after which the mixtures are ground or milled. Comminuted powders are then calcined, sometimes after compaction, and the firing sequence may be repeated several times with intermediate grinding stages. As for coprecipitation, impurities can be introduced into the ceramic from the grinding operation, grinding also results in angular-shaped powders.

Several problems are associated with mixing powders. High temperatures required for reaction between components can result in loss of volatile oxides, while milling may not comminute powders sufficiently for complete reaction to occur on calcination. It is difficult to obtain reproducible uniform distributions of material in ball-milled powders especially when one fraction is present in small amounts as occurs in electroceramics whose properties are often controlled by grain boundary phases containing minor quantities of additives[2]. The $YBa_2Cu_3O_{7-\delta}$ superconductor was synthesized by mixing Y_2O_3, $BaCO_3$ and CuO, grinding and heating at 1223K in air. Powder was then pressed into pellets, sintered in flowing O_2, cooled to 473K in O_2 and removed from the furnace.

Uniaxial Pressing

In uniaxial pressing a hard steel die is filled with either dry powder, or a powder containing up to several weight percent of H_2O, and a hard metal punch is driven into the die to form a coherent compact. Van der Waals forces cause aggregation of fine powders so that binders such as polyvinyl alcohol and lubricants are incorporated into them by, for example, spray-drying in order to improve their flow properties and homogeneity of the product. It is important that the unfired or green body has adequate strength for handling before the firing operation, during which organic additives are decomposed. Uniaxial pressing can be readily automated and is particularly suited for forming components with a simple shape such as flat discs and rings that can be produced to close dimensional tolerances, thus avoiding post-firing diamond machining operations.

Hot Uniaxial Pressing

Hot uniaxial pressing or hot-pressing involves simultaneous application of heat and pressure during sintering. A refractory die, usually graphite, is filled with powder, which after compaction, is heated in an inert atmosphere. Hot pressing produces higher density and smaller grain sizes at lower temperatures compared with uniaxial pressing and is particularly suited for fabrication of flat plates, blocks and cylinders. Stresses set up by the applied pressure on contacts between particles increase the driving force for sintering and remove the need for very fine particle sizes. Additives such as magnesium oxide and yttrium oxide, which are often used for Si_3N_4, allow achievement of theoretical density at lower temperatures. Theses sintering aids result in formation of a liquid phase and particle rearrangement because of capillary forces arising from the Laplace equation and by dissolution-recrystallization processes. However, advantages brought about by additives have to be offset by degradation in mechanical behavior of sintered components especially at high temperature because glassy and crystalline grain boundary phases derived from them often have inferior properties compared with the matrix[3].

Solid-State Sintering

The driving force for sintering is reduction in surface free energy associated with a decrease of surface area in powder compacts due to removal of solid-vapour interfaces. Vapour phase nucleation is describer by using the Kelvin equation, which is also applicable to mass-transport process in a consolidated powder. The vapour-pressure difference across a curved interface can enhance evaporation from particle surfaces and condensation at the neck between two particles, particularly for particle diameters of several micrometers or less, such as occur in ceramic fabrication. Although this evaporation-condensation process produces changes in pore shape and joins particles together, the centre-to-centre distance between particles remains constant so that shrinkage and densification do not occur. The driving force for mass transport by solid-state processes for ceramic powders with low vapour pressure is the difference in free energy between the neck region and surface of particles. As for the evaporation-condensation pathway, transport from surface to neck by surface and lattice diffusion does not cause densification. This is produced only by diffusion from the grain boundary between particles and from the bulk lattice. Covalent ceramics such as Si3N4 are more difficult to sinter to high density than ionic solids, for example Al_2O_3, because of lower atomic mobilities, although difficulties can be overcome by using very fine powders ca . 0.1μm diameter, high temperature and high pressure.

Impurities such as oxygen and chlorine in Si_3N_4 often migrate during sintering to grain boundaries where they reduce the interfacial surface energy and impair densification, creep behavior, oxidation resistance and high temperature strength.

New Words and Expressions

sintering	n.	烧结
porosity	n.	气孔率，多孔性
grain size		粒度，颗粒大小
microstructure	n.	显微结构
alumina	n.	氧化铝
bauxite	n.	铝土矿，（铁）矾土
impurity	n.	杂质，不纯物
gibbsite	n.	三水铝石(α-Al_2O_3·3H_2O)
bayerite	n.	三水铝石(β-Al_2O_3·3H_2O)
neutralization	n.	中和（作用，法）
supersaturation	n.	过饱和
crystallisation	n.	结晶（作用），晶化
deposit	v.	（使）沉积，涂，覆
inhomogeneity	n.	不（均）匀性，不同类（质），多相（性）
deleterious	adj.	有害的，有害杂质的
agglomerate	v.	（使）聚结，结块，成团；
	n., adj.	烧结块（的）附聚物（的）
grinding	n.	研磨，磨碎
oxalate	n.	草酸盐
intercalate	vt.	添加，插入
multicomponent	adj.	多成分的，多元的

91

calcine	v.	煅烧，烧成
grain boundary	n.	颗粒界面，晶界
pellet	n.	片，粒化（料），丸
binder	n.	黏结剂
polyvinyl	n., adj.	聚乙烯（的）
spray-drying	n.	喷雾干燥
green body	n.	生坯，未烧坯
yttrium	n.	钇
rearrangement	n.	重排
matrix	n.	基体，基质
shrinkage	n.	收缩（性，量，率）
impair	v.	削弱，损害
creep	n.	蠕变
annealing	n., adj.	退火，退火的

Notes

① 因为沉淀会产生团聚的粉体，因此研磨、干磨或者使用水或非水性液体的湿磨可用于减小粒径，以便粉末密实体可以烧结至接近理论密度。

② 在球磨制备粉体的情况下，难以得到可重复生产的均匀分布的粉料，尤其当电子陶瓷生产中一部分原料的用量很少时更是如此；电子陶瓷的性质常由含有少量添加剂的晶界相所控制。

③ 然而，引入添加剂所带来的优点不得不抵消烧结组分的机械性能下降的不足（尤其是在高温下），因为由添加剂产生的玻璃和晶界相常具有比基体差的性质。

Exercises

1. Translate the following sentence from English into Chinese.

Solid ceramic bodies are generally produced by using the process of powder compaction followed by firing at high temperature. Sintering or densification occurs during this heat treatment and is associated with joining together of particles, volume reduction, decrease in porosity and increase in grain size. The phase distribution or microstructure within the ceramic is developed during sintering and fabrication techniques used for shaping ceramics are described here. The aim of these techniques is to produce microstructures suitable for particular applications.

2. Translate the following expressions from Chinese into English.

(1) 退火和烧结温度

(2) 颗粒尺寸分布

(3) 颗粒的重排和团聚

(4) 喷雾干燥和煅烧

(5) 共沉淀和过饱和

Unit 12　Structure of Glass

The Structure of Glass

In spite of the world wide development of glass technology we still have found no definite answer to the question: what is glass? The following three different definitions are given to demonstrate how to describe the state of glass:

Glass is an inorganic product of a melt which solidifies without crystallizing;

Glass is an undercooled liquid with a very high viscosity;

Glass is an intermediate substance between the liquid and crystalline states. It consists of a crystal-like net word combined with each other randomly.

An early idea of the structure of glass was based on the concept of the term supercooled liquid. Molten glass was regarded as a solution of one oxide within another oxide, or rather a mutual solution of constituents[①] within each other. The molten liquid is cooled without crystallization to form a rigid body at room temperature.

The Network Theory

In recent years, the theory of the atomic structure of glass advanced by Zachariasen has become widely accepted. His random network theory assumes unit building blocks placed together in a random network manner. Our understanding of the constitution and the behavior of glasses is based on the descriptions of the structures of oxide glasses and on the conditions of glass formation as interpreted by a few pioneers in glass research. Tammann began to explore systematically the phenomena of the glassy state stating that the rate of cooling is most important for the understanding of the glassy state. Glasses are rigid solids and not liquids. In 1926, Goldschmidt presented his ideas on modern crystal chemistry.

A glass may resemble the crystal of the same composition with respect to the short range order, but its typical glass properties are the result of the lack of long range order. The ability of a molten substance to solidify on cooling without crystallization 96was explained on the basis of the geometry of the polyhedra, in particular of the ratio of the sizes of anions and cations. Thus, Goldschmidt introduced crystal chemical concepts into the field of glass technology. A decisive step in the development of glass structures was made by Zachariasen in 1932 who presented a picture of the atomic structure of vitreous silica in which the silicon atoms are surrounded by four oxygens in the same way as in the different structures of crystalline silica and silicates. The only difference between glass and crystal was the absence of periodicity. The continuous, random, three-dimensional structure shows the same short range order as the crystalline modifications of silica but without their long range order[②].

The introduction of alkali oxides into vitreous silica loosens its structure by decreasing the number of corners which each tetrahedron has to share with others[③]. This feature could account for the lower viscosity of an alkali silicate glass as compared to pure silica. The classification of the constituents of a glass into network forming oxides and those which modify the network was simple and useful. The "intermediates" were introduced years later. There was a nearly universal acceptance of Zachariasen' rules concerning glass formation. Wrrren and his school using X-ray techniques for determining the atomic structures of glasses agreed with Zachariasen's picture. The application of X-ray made by for the most important contribution to the present concept of the constitution of glass.

The network formers belong to a group of elements having an energy of the element-oxygen bond of 340 to 500 kJ/mol. The network-modifiers, for example Mg, Ca, Li, K, Na, Cd, and Cs have an ionic oxygen bond with a bonding energy of 40 to 250 kJ/mol. Their rates of diffusion are higher especially for the Me^+ ions. They break the continuous Si-O-Si network decreasing the viscosity of the melt at all temperatures. Me^{2+} ions act as a bridge between two oxygen atoms. They also break the network structure, but are less movable, influencing the flow of the melt less than Me^+ ions.

The main difference between a crystal and a glass is the kind of linkage of the tetrahedral. The crystalline structure repeats itself continuously in three dimensions, while in silica network the SiO_2 units are called glassformers. Such a glassformer determines the overall structure of the network. Commercial soda-silica and soda-lime-silica glasses contain other materials added to the silica glass. These materials are called network-modifiers, because they open the network up and introduce into it a number of oxygens larger than can be contained in the structure where all oxygens are bridges between two silicons. This produces some non-bridging oxygens which are connected to only one silicon and cause a breaking of the structure.

New Words and Expressions

solidify	v.	固化
undercooled	adj.	过冷的
supercooled	adj.	超冷的
rigid body	n.	刚性体
short range order		近程有序
long range order		长程有序
be surrounded by		被包围
periodicity	n.	周期律
net work former		网络形成体
net work-fodifier		网络调整体

Notes

① Mutual solution of constituents:组成的互溶体，把玻璃看成是过冷的液体。

② The continuous, random, three-dimensional structure shows the same short range order as the crystalline modifications of silica but without their long range order.
连续、随机和三维的结构具有和二氧化硅晶体相同的近程有序性，只是不具备相同的长程有序性。

③ The introduction of alkali oxides into vitreous silica loosens its structure by decreasing the number of corners which each tetrahedron has to share with others.

桥氧位于四面体的顶角，所以 corners 在这里指桥氧，整句可译成：玻璃态的二氧化硅中引入了碱金属之后，由于降低了由各个四面体共享的桥氧数，使结构变得松散。

Exercises

1. Translate the following sentence from English into Chinese.

An early idea of the structure of glass was based on the concept of the term supercooled liquid. Molten glass was regarded as a solution of one oxide within another oxide, or rather a mutual solution of constituent within each other. The molten liquid is cooled without crystallization to form a rigid body at room temperature.

2. Translate the following expressions from Chinese into English.

互溶体	玻璃态的	玻璃组成
网络调整体	中间体	网络结构
刚性体	碱金属	四面体

Part III　The Reading Materials

Unit 1　Hydration Mechanism

Tricalcium Silicate and Dicalcium silicate

The mechanism of hydration of individual cement components and that of cement itself has been a subject of much discussion and disagreement. In the earlier theory Le Chatelier explained the cementing action by dissolution of anhydrous compounds followed by the precipitation of interlocking crystalline hydrated compounds. Michealis considered that cohesion resulted from the formation and subsequent desiccation of the gel. In recent years the topochemical or solid-state mechanism has been proposed.

In spite of a large amount of work, even the mechanism of hydration of C_3S, the major phase of cement is not clear. Any mechanism proposed to explain the hydrating behavior of C_3S should take into account the following steps through which the hydration proceeds. Five steps can be discerned from the isothermal conduction calorimetric studies(Figure 1-1).In the first stage, as soon as C_3S comes into contact with water there is a rapid evolution of heat and this ceases within 15~20 minutes. This stage is called pre-induction period. In the second stage the reaction rate is very slow and is known as dormant or induction period. This may extend for a few hours. At this stage the cement remains plastic and is workable. In the third stage the reaction occurs actively and accelerates with time reaching a maximum rate at the end of this accelerating period. Initial set occurs at about the time when the rate of reaction becomes vigorous. The final set occurs before the end of third stage. In the fourth stage there is slow deceleration. An understanding of the first two stages of the reaction has a very important bearing on the subsequent hydration behavior of the sample. The admixtures can influence these stapes.

The processes that occur during the five stages are as follows. In the first stage as soon as C_3S comes into contact with water it releases calcium and hydroxyl ions into the solution. In the second stage the dissolution continues and PH reaches a high value of 12.5. Not much silica dissolution occurs at this stage. After a certain critical value of calcium and hydroxide ions is reached there is a rapid crystallization of CH and C-S-H followed by a rapid reaction. In the fourth stage there is a continuous formation of hydration products. At the final stage there is only a slow formation of products and at this stage the reaction is diffusion controlled. Comparatively less attention has been accorded to stages III, IV and V than to stages I and II.

Many publications have been devoted to explain the mechanism causing the induction period and its subsequent termination. It is generally thought that initially a reaction product forms on the C_3S surface that slows down the reaction. The renewed reaction is caused by the disruption of surface layer. According to Stein and Stevels the first hydrate has a high C/S ratio

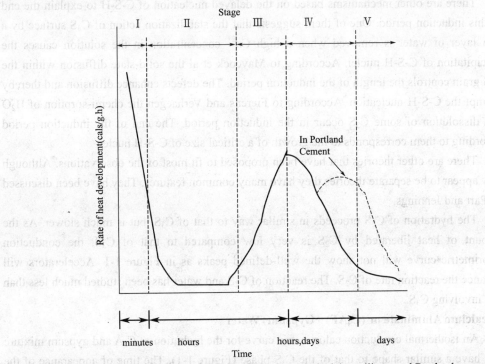

Figure 1-1　Rate of heat development during the hydration of tricalcium silicate and Portland cement

of about 3, and it transforms into a lower C/S ratio of about 0.8~1.5 through loss of calcium ions into solution. The second product has the property of allowing ionic species to pass through it thus enabling a rapid reaction. The conversion of the first to the second hydrate is thought to be a nucleation and growth process. Although this theory is consistent with many observations there are others that do not conform to this theory. They are: the C/S ratio of the product is lower than what has been reported, the protective layer may not be continuous, the product is a delicate film that easily peels away from the surface and the early dissolution may or may not be congruent.

The end of the induction period has been explained by the delayed nucleation of CH. It is generally observed that the rapid growth of crystalline CH and the fall of calcium ions in solution occur at the end of the induction period. This suggested that the precipitation of CH is related to the start of the acceleratory stage. If precipitation of CH triggers the reaction, then additional Ca ions should accelerate the reaction, unless it is poisoned. Addition of saturated lime is known to retard the reaction. Also it does not explain the accelerated formation of C-S-H. Tadros et al found the zeta potential of the hydrating C_3S surface to be positive, indicating the possibility of the chemisorption of Ca ions on the surface resulting in a layer that could serve as a barrier between C_3S and water. During the precipitation of $Ca(OH)_2$ it is though that Ca^{2+} from the solution is removed (which will in turn trigger the removal of Ca^{2+} from the barrier) and the reaction is accelerated.

There are other mechanisms based on the delayed nucleation of C-S-H to explain the end of this induction period. One of them suggests that the stabilization action of C_3S surface by a thin layer of water is removed when a high Ca^{2+} concentration in the solution causes the precipitation of C-S-H nuclei. According to Maycock et al the solid-state diffusion within the C_3S grain controls the length of the induction period. The defects enhance diffusion and thereby prompt the C-S-H nucleation. According to Fierens and Verhaegen the chemi-sorption of H_2O and dissolution of some C_3S occur in the induction period. The end of the induction period according to them corresponds to the growth of a critical size of C-S-H nuclei.

There are other theories that have been proposed to fit most of the observations. Although they appear to be separate theories they have many common features. They have been discussed by Part and Jennings.

The hydration of C_2S proceeds in similar way to that of C_3S, but is much slower. As the amount of heat liberated by C_2S is very low compared to that of C_3S, the conduction calorimetric curve will not show the well-defined peaks as in Figure 1-1 .Accelerators will enhance the reaction rate of C_2S. The reaction of C_2S and water has been studied much less than that involving C_3S.

Tricalcium Aluminate or (C_4AF) +Gypsum+Water

An isothermal conduction calorimetric curve for the hydration of C_3A and gypsum mixture will have a similar shape to that of the C_3S phase (Figure 1-1). The time of appearance of the peaks and their magnitude are, however, not the same. The common view for the explanation of the retardation of the retardation of C_3A hydration by gypsum is that a fine-grained ettringite forming on C_3A retards the hydration. This layer thickens in the induction period and bursts and reforms during this period. When all sulfates are consumed the ettringite reacts with C_3A with the formation of mono-sulfoaluminate hydrate. This conversion will occur in cements within 12~36 hours with an exothermic peak. Addition of some admixtures may accelerate or delay this conversion. It has also been suggested that ettringite may not *per se* influence the induction period and that absorption of sulfate ions on the positively charged C_3A retards the hydration. It has also been suggested that osmotic pressure may be involved in the rupture of ettringite needles. This theory is based on the observation of hollow needles in the C_3A-Gypsum-H_2O system. Rupture of ettringite allows transfer of Al ions in the aqueous phase with quick formation of hollow needles through which more Al^{3+} can travel.

The C_4AF phase forms the same sequence of products as C_3A. Gypsum retards C_4AF hydration more efficiently than it does C_3A. Although cements high in C_3A are prone to sulfate attack, those with high C_4AF are not. In high C_4AF cements, ettringite may not form from the low sulfoaluminate possible because of the substitution of iron in the momosulfate. It is also possibility is that the sulfoaluminate phase is produced in such a way that it does not create crystalline growth pressures.

Portland cement

The mechanisms that have already been described for pure cement compounds form a basis for the study of the hydration mechanism of Portland cement. The conduction calorimetric curves of C_3S and Portland cement are similar except Portland cement may yield a third peak for the formation of monosulfate hydrate. The detailed influence of C_3A and C_4AF on the hydration of C_3S and C_2S in cement is yet to be worked out. The delayed nucleation models and the protective layer models, talking into account the possible interactions, has been reviewed. Although the initial process is not clear for C_3S (in cements) it appears that C_3A hydration products form through solution and topochemical processes.

Unit 2   Alkali-aggregate Reactions

Although all aggregates can be considered reactive, only those that actually cause damage to concrete are of concern in concrete practice, Alkali-aggregate reaction became a noticeable problem when cements with higher alkali contents were used. Such cements became more common because of more economical methods of cement production. Other factors include the widespread use of aggregates of marginal quality and the production of high strength concrete.

The alkali-aggregate reaction in concrete may manifest itself as a map of cracking on the exposed surface, although other reactions may also produce such failures. The alkali-aggregate reaction, known as the alkali-silica type, may promote exudation of a water gel, which dries to a white deposit. These manifestations may appear only after months or even years.

Several tests exist. The petrographic method, according to ASTM C295, is used for characterization purposes. The rock cylinder method (ASTM C586) examines the potential alkali reactivity of carbonate rocks used as aggregate. ASTM C227 is a mortar bar test for potential reactivity due to the presence of silica. The concrete prism test, specified in CSAA23.2-14A, reflects the actual behavior of concrete.

Alkalis: Alkalis exist in soluble form in Portland cement. The water-soluble alkali content, determined according to the ASTM C114-77 method, varies between 10% and 60% of the total amount. The soluble portion is, to a large extent, present as sulfate and is mainly derived from the fuel used in cement production. Water-insoluble alkalis are derived from clay and other siliceous components of the raw mix. In the clinker, they are present in combined form with the cement components.

After the initial stages of reaction and within a few days, the solution contains as many hydroxide ions as the combined concentration of potassium and sodium ions, since most of the sulface ions combine with the C_3A component.

Generally, the total amount of K_2O and Na_2O in cement (expressed as Na_2O equivalent) does not exceed 1.0%.Cements containing less than 0.6% Na_2O equivalent are commonly termed low alkali cements.

Types of Alkali-aggregate Reactions: There are three types of alkali-aggregate reactions that have been detected by works, although that involving silicates has not received general recognition.

(a) Alkali-silica Reaction: The aggregates involved in this type of reaction are those containing opal, vitreous volcanic rocks, and those containing more than 95% silica. Silica existing in a microcrystalline phase is responsible for this type of reaction. Quartz is relatively unreactive due to the orderly arrangement of the Si-O tetrahedron, whereas the reactive form of silica comprise a randomly arranged tetrahedral network.

The expansion of mortar bars containing opal typifies the alkali-silica reaction. In the reaction, NaOH appears to be more aggressive than KOH, and the presence of moisture is essential to the expansion. The maximum expansion seems to depend on a certain proportion of the reactive material in aggregate, known as the "pessimum" content. This proportion is about 3.5% for a reactive aggregate, like opal, and may be 10%~20%, or even higher, for less reactive materials depending on the alkali content of the cement.

Currently, two theories are considered to explain the alkali-silica expansive reaction, both being based on the properties of the reaction products. One theory attributes expansion to the uptake of water by the silica-gel product and the other to osmotic pressure effects.

(b) Alkali-carbonate Reaction: Certain types of carbonate rock, argillaceous dolomitic limestones and calcite dolostones containing meta-stable dolomitic and possible crypto-crystalline (adj.隐晶的) calcite are susceptible to reaction with alkalis. This type of reaction is different from the alkali-silica reaction because of the absence of characteristic reaction products normally detected by visual or microscopic methods. The expansive dolomites contain more $CaCO_3$ than the ideal 50% (mole) proportion and frequently contain illite and chlorite clay minerals. However, it is very unlikely that this reaction can account for the expansion of concrete or rock prisms exposed to alkali solutions. Swenson and Gillot postulated that because he dolomite crystals formed under high pressure that included clay (illite and chlorite) in such crystals were active and devoid of free water .The role of the dedolomitization reaction was considered important to the extent that it disrupted or removed the dolomite crystals so that moisture and solutions could interact with the clay fraction, resulting in the generation of swelling pressures.

(c)Alkali-silicate Reaction: This reaction has been proposed by Gillot. The rocks that produce this type of reaction are greywackes, argillite and Phyllis containing vermiculites. This reaction differs from others by showing very slow rate of expansion and by the absence of even very small amounts of minerals known to promote alkali-aggregate reaction. In some rocks, the presence of strained quartz may explain part of the expansion. In many instances phyllo-silicates present in the rocks have caused expansion. These silicates seem to exfoliate after alkali treatment, unlike other layer silicates. More detailed work is warranted before this type of reaction is established as one belonging to a new category.

Preventive Methods: Aside from the obvious method of avoiding the use of high alkali cement and reactive aggregates, one other major Method is a partial replacement of cement with pozzolans and/or blast-furnace Slag (20%~30%). Some pozzolans may contain substantial amounts of alkalis, however, and standard tests (ASTM C441) should be carried out to test the effectiveness of a pozzolan. The mechanism of action the pozzolan in preventing the alkali-aggregate reaction is not completely understood, but one possibility is that the amount of alkali in the mix is diluted. It has also been suggested that in the presence of a pozzolan, the nonswelling lime-alkali-silica complex forms in place of the swelling alkali-silicate gels. Another suggestion is that both pozzolan and blast-furnace slag produce very impermeable matrices and restrict the mobility of ions needed to enhance the deleterious reactions. The addition of pozzolans may not, however, be effective in controlling the alkali-carbonate

101

reactions.

In addition to the above, research has continued to discover an additive that can inhibit the alkali-aggregate expansion. McCoy and Caldwell have used about 1% lithium compounds to control expansive. Luginina and Mikhalev have suggested the addition of phosphates in the kiln to control the alkali-aggregate expansion. Mehta studied the effect of various chemical additions to systems containing high alkali cement and reactive aggregates. The effectiveness of anions in reducing the expansion was in the order $NO_3^->CO_3^{2-}>Cl^->SO_4^{2-}$. Barium salts have also been tried in combination with gypsum-free ground clinker for controlling the alkali-aggregate reactions.

Other methods that should be considered are (i) beneficiation of the aggregate, (ii) dilution of the reactive aggregate with a nonreactive aggregate, (iii) reducing the cement content of the mix, (iv) designing of structure to minimize the surface subjected to wetting, (v) ensure good drainage so that water does not pond on the structure.

Words and Expressions

Alkali-aggregate reaction	*abbr.*	AAR-碱-骨料反应
marginal	*adj.*	临界的，最低限的
exudation	*n.*	渗出
petrographic	*adj.*	[地]岩相学的
opal	*n.*	[矿]蛋白质
vitreous	*adj.*	玻璃质的
volcanic	*adj.*	火山的
microcrystalline	*adj.*	微晶的
tetrahedron	*n.*	四面体
pessimum	*n.*	最不利
uptake	*n.*	吸收
osmotic	*adj.*	渗透的
dolomitic	*adj.*	[矿]含白云石的
calcite	*n.*	[矿]方解石
dolostone	*n.*	白云岩
dolomites	*n.*	[矿]白云石
illite	*n.*	[矿]伊利石
chlorite	*n.*	[化]亚氯酸盐，绿泥石
dedolomitization	*n.*	[地质]脱白云石作用
greywacke	*n.*	[地]杂砂岩
argillite	*n.*	硅质黏土岩
Phyllis	*n.*	[地]千枚岩
vermiculite	*n.*	[矿]蛭石
phyllo		薄夹层
exfoliate	*vt.*	片层剥落
Slag		高炉炉渣

Unit 3   Workability, Setting, Bleeding and Segregation

Workability

The quality of fresh concrete is determined by the ease and homogeneity with which it can be mixed, transported, compacted and finished. It has also been defined as the amount of internal work necessary to produce full compaction. The rheological behavior of concrete is related to the rheological terms such as plasticity and visco-elasticity of cement paste. As the workability depends on the conditions of placement, the intended use will determine whether the concrete has the required workability. A good workable concrete should not exhibit excessive bleeding and segregation. Thus workability includes properties such as flowability, moldability, cohesiveness and compactibility. One of the main factors affecting workability is the water content in the concrete mix. A harsh concrete becomes workable by the addition of water. Workability may also be improved by the addition of plasticizers and air entraining agents. The factors that affect workability include quantities of paste and aggregates, plasticity of the cement paste, maximum size and grading of aggregates and shape and surface characteristics of the aggregates.

Another term that has been used to describe the state of fresh concrete is consistency or fluidity. It describes the ease with which a substance flows. It is loosely related to an import component of workability. The term consistency is sometimes used to describe the degree of wetness of concrete. Wet concrete is more workable than the dry concrete. A concrete having the same consistency may however have different workability characteristics. The ASTM C-187 and Canadian Standard CSA CAN 3-A5 measure the consistency of cement paste by a Vicat apparatus consisting of a needle of diameter 1 mm with a plunger of diameter 10 mm. The pasties considered to have normal consistency when the rod settles to point to (10 ± 1) mm below the original surface in 30 secs after being released. In the determination of setting and soundness of cement paste the material should be made to normal consistency requirements.

Although several methods have been suggested to determine workability, none is capable of measuring this property directly. It is therefore usual to measure some type of consistency as an index of workability. The most extensively used test is the slump test. This method is described in ASTM C142-78. The slump test uses a frustum of cone 30 mm (12 in) high. Concrete is filled in the come and the cone is lifted slowly and the decrease in height of the center of the slump of 75~100 mm (3~4 in) is sufficient for placement in forms. Another method called the "Compacting Factor Test" is based on the measurement of the density ratio (the ratio of density actually achieved in the test to the density of the fully compacted concrete).

This method is described in BS 1881, Part 2, 1970 and in ACI 2113-75. Another method called the "Ball Penetration Test" is described in ASTM C360. This method is based on measuring the penetration of 150 mm (6 in) diameter steel cylinder with a hemispherically shaped bottom weighing 13.6 kg (30 lb). The ratio of slump to the penetration of the ball is about $1.5\sim2$. In the "Remolding Test" developed by Powers, workability is assessed on the basis of the effort require in changing the shape of the concrete. The" Vebe Test" is similar to the remolding test except that the inner ring is omitted and compaction is achieved by vibration instead of rolling. In addition to the above there are other methods that have been used. They include Vebe consistometer, German Flow Table, Nasser's K-probe and Tattersall's two points test. All these tests these tests attempt to measure workability and they are not comparable. No ideal test for workability has been developed as yet.

Setting

The stiffening times of cement paste or mortar fraction are determined by setting times. The setting characteristics are assessed by "initial set" and "final set". When the concrete attains the stage of initial set it can no longer be properly handled and placed. The final set corresponds to the stage at which hardening begins. At the time of the initial set the concrete will have exhibited a measurable loss of slump. Admixtures may influence the setting times.

At the time of initial set of cement paste the hydration of C_3S will have just started. According to some investigators, the recrystallization of ettringite is the major contributing factor to the initial set. The final set occurs before the paste shows the maximum rate of heat development, i.e., before the end of the 3rd stage.

Concrete also exhibits false or flash set. When stiffening occurs due to the presence of partially dehydrated gypsum, false set is noticed. Workability is restored by remixing. False set may also be caused by excessive formation of ettringite especially in the presence of some retarders. The formation of syngenite is reported to cause false set in some instances.

Concrete may exhibit flash set due to the reaction of C_3A, forming calcium aluminate hydrates and monosulfate hydrate. Workability will not be restored by remixing when flash set occurs.

The setting time of cement can be determined by Gillmore (ASTM C 266) or the Vicat apparatus (ASTMC 191). In the Gillmore method a pat of cement paste with 3 in diameter and 1/2 in thickness is formed on a glass plate and is subjected to indentation by the needle. For the initial set the needle weighing 1/4 lb with 1/12 in diameter is used while for final set the corresponding figure is 1 lb and 1/24 in diameter. The initial set occurs when the pat with bear, without appreciable indentation, the initial Gillmore needle. Similarly the final set is determined by the Gillmore needle. All standard ASTM cements should conform to an initial setting time of not less than 60 mins and final setting time of not more than 10 hrs. The corresponding times using the Vicat needle are 45 mins. and 8 hrs.

The Vicat apparatus is similar to the method described above except that there are sight differences in the needle weight and diameter, and the dimensions of the cement paste. In this method the initial setting time occurs when a penetration of 25 mm is obtained. At the time of final set the needle should not sink visibly into the paste. The Canadian standards method CSA CAN3-A5 specifies only the initial setting times. The Vicat apparatus is also specified by British Standard BS12:1978.

The setting of concrete is determined by using the mortar contained in it. A penetrometer is used for determining the initial and final setting times of mortar. A needle of appropriate size has to be used. The force require to penetrate 1 in depth is noted. The force divided by the area of the bearing surface of the needle yields the penetration resistance. The initial setting time is the elapsed time after the initial contact of cement and water required for the mortar sieved from the concrete to reach a penetration resistance of 500 lb/ sq in (3.5 MPa). The corresponding resistance for final setting time is 4000lb/ in (14MPa).

Bleeding and Segregation

In freshly placed concrete that is still plastic, settlement of solids is followed by the formation of a layer of water on the surface. This is known as bleeding or water gain. In lean mixes localize channels develop and the seepage of water transports some particles to the surface. Bleeding may thus give rise to "laitance", a layer of weak nondurable material containing diluted cement paste and fines from the aggregate. If bleeding occurs by uniform seepage of water no undesirable effects result and such a bleeding is known as "normal bleeding". Bleeding is not necessarily harmful. If undisturbed, the water evaporates so that effective water-cement ratio is lowered with a resultant increase in strength.

The amount of bleeding can be reduced by using proper amounts of fines, high alkali or C_3A contents, increasing cement content and admixtures such as pozzolana, calcium chloride or air entraining admixtures. Bleeding characteristics are measured by bleeding rate or bleeding capacity applying the ASTM C232 standard. In this method the relative amount of mix water that appears on the surface of concrete placed in a cylindrical container is measured. At specified intervals the water accumulating on the surface is determined until bleeding ceases. The top surface of concrete subsides during bleeding causing what is known as "plastic shrinkage".

During the handling of concrete mixture there may be some separation of coarse aggregates form the mixture resulting in a nonuniform concrete mass. This is known as segregation. Segregation may lead to flaws in the final product and honeycombing may occur in some instance. Segregation may result during hand ling, placing, vibrating or finishing operations. The primary cause of segregation is the differences in the size of the maximum size and amount of aggregate. This problem can be controlled by proper grading of the constituents and handing.

There is no standard procedure developed for measuring segregation. For over-vibrated concrete, proneness to segregation can be assessed by vibrating a concrete cube for about 10 minutes, stripping it and observing the distribution of coarse aggregate.

Words and Expressions

homogeneity	n.	均一性
rheological	adj.	[物] 流变学的
consistency	n.	稠度
slump	n.	坍落度
Vebe	n.	维勃
ettringite	n.	钙矾石
syngenite	n.	[矿] 钾石膏
penetrometer	n.	穿透仪
laitance	n.	浮浆层
honeycombing	n.	蜂窝

Unit 4　Concrete Science

Design and Control of Concrete

In this section, the basic requirements for concrete, curing techniques, strength gained by curing and slump testing, are examined. These characteristics are fundamental to all types of concrete.

The Basic Requirements for Concrete

The basic requirements for concrete are conveniently considered at two stages in its life.

In its hardened state (in the completed structure) the concrete should have adequate durability, the required strength and also the desired surface finish.

In its plastic state, or the stage during which it is to be handled, placed and compacted in its finial form, it should be sufficiently workable for the required properties in its hardened state to be achieved with the facilities available on site. This means that:

(1) The concrete should be sufficiently fluid for it to be able to flow into and fill all parts of the formwork, or mould, into which it is placed.

(2) It should do so without any segregation, or separation, of the constituent materials while being handled from the mixer or during placing.

(3) It must be possible to fully compact the concrete when placed in position.

(4) It must be possible to obtain the required surface finish.

If concrete does not have the required workability in its plastic state, it will not be possible to produce concrete with the required properties in its hardened state. The dependence of both durability and strength on the degree of compaction has been noted earlier. Segregation results in variations in the mix proportions throughout the bulk of the concrete and this inevitably means that in some parts the coarser aggregate particles will predominate. This precludes the possibility of full compaction since there is insufficient mortar to fill the voids between the coarser particles in these zones. This results in what is descriptively known as honeycombing on the surface of the hardened concrete with reduced durability and strength as well as unacceptable surface finish.

Curing Techniques and Strength Gained by Curing

As long as conditions are favorable for continued hydration of cement, concrete will continues to improve its various properties, such as strength, water-tightness, wear resistance, freeze and thaw resistance, volume, etc. The conditions needed to accomplish these improvements, called the *curing medium*, are (1) the presence of moisture and (2) a favorable temperature. Recall that hydration continues as long as moisture is present in and around cement. If it evaporates, hydration stops but may be started again if moisture is replenished. Recall also that heat of hydration is high where temperatures are high and low near freezing temperatures. It therefore follows that concrete-curing methods must supply or maintain the presence of

107

moisture and provide favorable temperatures for continued curing.

Curing methods that supply additional moisture to the surface of concrete during the early hardening period include ponding, sprinkling, and the application of wet coverings. Methods that prevent loss of moisture from the concrete by sealing the surface may include the use of waterproof papers, plastic sheets, liquid-membrane-forming compounds, and forms left in place. Methods that accelerate strength gained by supplying heat and moisture to the concrete are accomplished with live steam or heating coil.

Testing for Slump

Slump is the amount of reduction in height of a cylinder of freshly made concrete, measured in inches or millimeters, when the cylinder's mold is removed. If a cylinder of fresh concrete is taken from every truck load (batch) and the slump is the same, then control of the mixture has been done properly. This indicates that there were no changes in materials, mix proportions, or water content. If slumps are different between batches where one slump more than another, excess water probably is the cause. A slump less than average value means a stiff mixture. In any use of concrete requiring more than one batch, the slump should be uniform.

Generally slump can be controlled by the percentage of water added to a mixture. An increase or a decrease of 3 percent usually alters the slump about 1 in. However, care must be taken not to upset the water-cement ratio.

As a general guideline, slumps range from 1 in to not more than 6 in. Some representative examples are listed in Table 4-1.

Table 4-1   Typical slumps for concrete by use

Types of construction	Slump(in.)	
	Maximum	Minimum
Reinforced foundation wall and footing	3	1
Unreinforced footings, caissons, and substructure walls	3	1
Reinforced slabs, beams, and walls	4	1
Building columns	4	1
Bridge decks	3	2
Pavements	2	1
Sidewalks, driveways, and slabs on the ground	4	2
Heavy mass construction	2	1

Source: "Design and Control of Concrete Mixture" Portland Cement Association, Skokie, III, 1968, Table II. Typical slump ranges for various types of construction.

Unit 5   Concrete as a Structural Material

In an article published by the Scientific American in April 1964, S. Brunauer and L.E. Copeland, two eminent scientists in the field of cement and concrete, wrote: The most widely used construction material is concrete, commonly made by mixing Portland cement with sand, crushed rock, and water. Last year in the U.S. 63 million tons of Portland cement was converted into 500 million tons of concrete, five times the consumption by weight of steel. In many countries the ratio of concrete consumption to steel consumption exceeds ten to one. The total world consumption of concrete last year is estimated at three billion tons, or one ton for every living human being. Man consumes no material except water in such tremendous quantities.

Today, the rate at which concrete is used is much higher than it was 40 years ago. It is estimated that the present consumption of concrete in the world is 11 billion metric tonnes every year. Concrete is neither as strong nor as tough as steel, so why is it the most widely used engineering material? There are at least three primary reasons.

First, concrete possesses excellent resistance to water. Unlike wood and ordinary steel, the ability of concrete to withstand the action of water without serious deterioration makes it an ideal material for building structures to control, store, and transport water. In fact, some of the earliest known applications of the material consisted of aqueducts and waterfront retaining walls constructed by the Romans. The use of plain concrete for dams, canal linings, and pavements is now a common sight almost everywhere in the world.

Structural elements exposed to moisture, such as piles, foundations, footings, floors, beams, columns, roofs, exterior walls, and pipes, are frequently built with reinforced and prestressed concrete. Reinforced concrete is a concrete usually containing steel bars, which is designed on the assumption that the two materials act together in resisting tensile forces. With prestressed concrete by tensioning the steel tendons, a precompression is introduced such that the tensile stresses during service are counteracted to prevent cracking. Large amounts of concrete find their way into reinforced or prestressed structural elements. The durability of concrete to aggressive waters is responsible for the fact that its use has been extended to severe industrial and natural environ ments.

The second reason for the widespread use of concrete is the ease with which structural concrete elements can be formed into a variety of shapes and sizes. This is because freshly made concrete is of a plastic consistency, which enables the material to flow into prefabricated formwork. After a number of hours when the concrete has solidified and hardened to a strong mass, the formwork can be removed for reuse.

The third reason for the popularity of concrete with engineers is that it is usually the cheapest and most readily available material on the job. The principal components for making concrete, namely aggregate, water, and Portland cement are relatively inexpensive and are

109

commonly available in most parts of the world. Depending on the components' transportation cost, in certain geographical locations the price of concrete may be as high as U.S. $75 to $100 per cubic meter, at others it may be as low as U.S. $60 to $70 per cubic meter. Some of the considerations that favor the use of concrete over steel as the construction material of choice are as follows:

Maintenance. Concrete does not corrode, needs no surface treatment, and its strength increases with time; therefore, concrete structures require much less maintenance. Steel structures, on the other hand, are susceptible to rather heavy corrosion in offshore environments, require costly surface treatment and other methods of protection, and entail considerable maintenance and repair costs.

Fire resistance. The fire resistance of concrete is perhaps the most important single aspect of offshore safety and, at the same time, the area in which the advantages of concrete are most evident. Since an adequate concrete cover on reinforcement or tendons is required for structural integrity in reinforced and prestressed concrete structures, the protection against failure due to excessive heat is provided at the same time.

Resistance to cyclic loading. The fatigue strength of steel structures is greatly influenced by local stress fields in welded joints, corrosion pitting, and sudden changes in geometry, such as from thin web to thick frame connections. In most codes of practice, the allowable concrete stresses are limited to about 50 percent of the ultimate strength; thus the fatigue strength of concrete is generally not a problem.

Types of Concrete

Based on unit weight, concrete can be classified into three broad categories. Concrete containing natural sand and gravel or crushed-rock aggregates, generally weighing about 2400 kg/m³ (4000 lb/yd³), is called normal-weight concrete, and it is the most commonly used concrete for structural purposes. For applications where a higher strength-to-weight ratio is desired, it is possible to reduce the unit weight of concrete by using natural or pyro-processed aggregates with lower bulk density. The term lightweight concrete is used for concrete that weighs less than about 1800 kg/m³ (3000 lb/yd³).

Heavyweight concrete, used for radiation shielding, is a concrete produced from high-density aggregates and generally weighs more than 3200 kg/m³ (5300 lb/yd³). Strength grading of cements and concrete is prevalent in Europe and many other countries but is not practiced in the United States. However, from standpoint of distinct differences in the microstructure-property relationships, which will be discussed later, it is useful to divide concrete into three general categories based on compressive strength:

Low-strength concrete:

- Less than 20 MPa (3000 psi)
- Moderate-strength concrete: 20 to 40 MPa (3000 to 6000 psi)
- High-strength concrete: more than 40 MPa (6000 psi).

Moderate-strength concrete also referred to as ordinary or normal concrete is used for most structural work. High-strength concrete is used for special applications. It is not possible here to list all concrete types. There are numerous modified concretes which are appropriately named: for example, fiber-reinforced concrete, expansive-cement concrete, and latex-modified concrete.

Typical proportions of materials for producing low-strength, moderate-strength, and high-strength concrete mixtures with normal-weight aggregate. The influence of the cement paste content and water-cement ratio on the strength of concrete is obvious.

Unit 6 Ceramic Materials: Definitions

If you look in any introductory materials science book you will find that one of the first sections describes the classification scheme. In classical materials science, materials are grouped into five categories: metals, polymers, ceramics, semiconductors, and composites. The first three are based primarily on the nature of the interatomic bonding, the fourth on the materials conductivity, and the last on the materials structure—not a very consistent start.

Metals, both pure and alloyed, consist of atoms held together by the delocalized electrons that overcome the mutual repulsion between the ion cores. Many main-group elements and all the transition and inner transition elements are metals. They also include alloys—combinations of metallic elements or metallic and nonmetallic elements (such as in steel, which is an alloy of primarily Fe and C). Some commercial steels, such as many tool steels, contain ceramics. These are the carbides (e.g., Fe_3C and W_6C) that produce the hardening and enhance wear resistance, but also make it more brittle. The delocalized electrons give metals many of their characteristic properties (e.g., good thermal and electrical conductivity). It is because of their bonding that many metals have close packed structures and deform plastically at room temperature.

Polymers are macromolecules formed by covalent bonding of many simpler molecular units called mers. Most polymers are organic compounds based on carbon, hydrogen, and other nonmetals such as sulfur and chlorine. The bonding between the molecular chains determines many of their properties. Cross-linking of the chains is the key to the vulcanization process that turned rubber from an interesting but not very useful material into, for example, tires that made traveling by bicycle much more comfortable and were important in the production of the automobile. The terms "polymer" and "plastic" are often used interchangeably. However, many of the plastics with which we are familiar are actually combinations of polymers, and often include fillers and other additives to give the desired properties and appearance.

Ceramics are usually associated with "mixed" bonding—a combination of covalent, ionic, and sometimes metallic. They consist of arrays of interconnected atoms; there are no discrete molecules. This characteristic distinguishes ceramics from molecular solids such as iodine crystals (composed of discrete I_2 molecules) and paraffin wax (composed of long-chain alkane molecules). It also excludes ice, which is composed of discrete H_2O molecules and often behaves just like many ceramics. The majority of ceramics are compounds of metals or metalloids and nonmetals. Most frequently they are oxides, nitrides, and carbides. However, we also classify diamond and graphite as ceramics. These forms of carbon are inorganic in the most basic meaning of the term: they were not prepared from the living organism. Richerson (2000) says "most solid materials that aren't metal, plastic, or derived from plants or animals are ceramics."

Semiconductors are the only class of material based on a property. They are usually

112

defined as having electrical conductivity between that of a good conductor and an insulator. The conductivity is strongly dependent upon the presence of small amounts of impurities—the key to making integrated circuits. Semiconductors with wide band gaps (greater than about 3 eV) such as silicon carbide and boron nitride are becoming of increasing importance for hightemperature electronics, for example, SiC diodes are of interest for sensors in fuel cells. In the early days of semiconductor technology such materials would have been regarded as insulators. Gallium nitride (GaN), a blue–green laser diode material, is another ceramic that has a wide band gap.

Composites are combinations of more than one material or phase. Ceramics are used in many composites, often for reinforcement. For example, one of the reasons a B-2 stealth bomber is stealthy is that it contains over 22 tons of carbon/epoxy composite. In some composites the ceramic is acting as the matrix (ceramic matrix composites or CMCs). An early example of a CMC dating back over 9000 years is brick. These often consisted of a fired clay body reinforced with straw. Clay is an important ceramic and the backbone of the traditional ceramic industry. In concrete, both the matrix (cement) and the reinforcement (aggregate) are ceramics.

The most widely accepted definition of a ceramic is given by Kingery et al. (1976): "A ceramic is a nonmetallic, inorganic solid." Thus all inorganic semiconductors are ceramics. By definition, a material ceases to be a ceramic when it is melted. At the opposite extreme, if we cool some ceramics enough they become superconductors. All the so-called high-temperature superconductors (HTSC) (ones that lose all electrical resistance at liquidnitrogen temperatures) are ceramics. Trickier is glass such as used in windows and optical fibers. Glass fulfills the standard definition of a solid—it has its own fixed shape—but it is usually a supercooled liquid. This property becomes evident at high temperatures when it undergoes viscous deformation. Glasses are clearly special ceramics. We may crystallize certain glasses to make glass–ceramics such as those found in Corningware. This process is referred to as "ceramming" the glass, i.e., making it into a ceramic. We stand by Kingery's definition and have to live with some confusion. We thus define ceramics in terms of what they are not.

It is also not possible to define ceramics, or indeed any class of material, in terms of specific properties.

_ We cannot say "ceramics are brittle" because some can be superplastically deformed and some metals can be more brittle: a rubber hose or banana at 77 K shatters under a hammer.

_ We cannot say "ceramics are insulators" unless we put a value on the band gap (E_g) where a material is not a semiconductor.

_ We cannot say "ceramics are poor conductors of heat" because diamond has the highest thermal conductivity of any known material.

Before we leave this section let us consider a little history. The word ceramic is derived from the Greek keramos, which means "potter's clay" or "pottery." Its origin is a Sanskrit term meaning "to burn." So the early Greeks used "keramos" when describing products obtained by heating clay-containing materials. The term has long included all products made from fired clay, for example, bricks, fireclay refractories, sanitaryware, and tableware.

In 1822, silica refractories were first made. Although they contained no clay the traditional ceramic process of shaping, drying, and firing was used to make them. So the term "ceramic," while retaining its original sense of a product made from clay, began to include other products made by the same manufacturing process. The field of ceramics (broader than the materials themselves) can be defined as the art and science of making and using solid articles that contain as their essential component a ceramic. This definition covers the purification of raw materials, the study and production of the chemical compounds concerned, their formation into components, and the study of structure, composition, and properties.

Unit 7 the Introduction of Ceramic

General Properties

Ceramics generally have specific properties associated with them although, as we just noted, this can be a misleading approach to defining a class of material. However, we will look at some properties and see how closely they match our expectations of what constitutes a ceramic.

Brittleness. This probably comes from personal experiences such as dropping a glass beaker or a dinner plate. The reason that the majority of ceramics are brittle is the mixed ionic-covalent bonding that holds the constituent atoms together. At high temperatures (above the glass transition temperature) glass no longer behaves in a brittle manner; it behaves as a viscous liquid. That is why it is easy to form glass into intricate shapes. So what we can say is that most ceramics are brittle at room temperature but not necessarily at elevated temperatures.

Poor electrical and thermal conduction. The valence electrons are tied up in bonds, and are not free as they are in metals. In metals it is the free electrons—the electron gas—that determines many of their electrical and thermal properties. Diamond, which we classified as a ceramic in Section 1.1, has the highest thermal conductivity of any known material. The conduction mechanism is due to phonons, not electrons, as we describe in Chapter 34.

Ceramics can also have high electrical conductivity: (1) the oxide ceramic, ReO_3, has an electrical conductivity at room temperature similar to that of Cu (2) the mixed oxide $YBa_2Cu_3O_7$ is an HTSC; it has zero resistivity below 92 K. These are two examples that contradict the conventional wisdom when it comes to ceramics.

Compressive strength. Ceramics are stronger in compression than in tension, whereas metals have comparable tensile and compressive strengths. This difference is important when we use ceramic components for load-bearing applications. It is necessary to consider the stress distributions in the ceramic to ensure that they are compressive. An important example is in the design of concrete bridges—the concrete, a CMC, must be kept in compression. Ceramics generally have low toughness, although combining them in composites can dramatically improve this property.

Chemical insensitivity. A large number of ceramics are stable in both harsh chemical and thermal environments. Pyrex glass is used widely in chemistry laboratories specifically because it is resistant to many corrosive chemicals, stable at high temperatures (it does not soften until 1100 K), and is resistant to thermal shock because of its low coefficient of thermal expansion (33×10^{-7} K^{-1}). It is also widely used in bakeware.

Transparent. Many ceramics are transparent because they have a large E_g. Examples include sapphire watch covers, precious stones, and optical fibers. Glass optical fibers have a percent transmission >96%km^{-1}. Metals are transparent to visible light only when they are very thin, typically less than 0.1 μm.

Although it is always possible to find at least one ceramic that shows atypical behavior, the properties we have mentioned here are in many cases different from those shown by metals and polymers.

Types of Ceramic and Their Applications

Using the definition given in Section 7.1 you can see that large numbers of materials are ceramics. The applications for these materials are diverse, from bricks and tiles to electronic and magnetic components. These applications use the wide range of properties exhibited by ceramics.

Some of these properties are listed in Table 7-1 together with examples of specific ceramics and applications. Each of these areas will be covered in more detail later. The functions of ceramic products are dependent on their chemical composition and microstructure, which determines their properties. It is the interrelationship between structure and properties that is a key element of materials science and engineering.

Table 7-1 properties and applications of some specific ceramics

Property	Example	Application
Electrical	$Bi2Ru_2O_7$ Doped ZrO_2 Indium tin oxide (ITO) SiC $YBaCuO_7$ SnO_2	Conductive component in thick-fi lm resistors Electrolyte in solid-oxide fuel cells Transparent electrode Furnace elements for resistive heating Superconducting quantum interference devices (SQUIDs) Electrodes for electric glass melting furnaces
Dielectric	$a\text{-}Al_2O_3$ $PbZr_{0.5}Ti_{0.5}O_3$ (PZT) SiO_2 $(Ba,Sr)TiO_3$ Lead magnesium niobate (PMN)	Spark plug insulator Micropumps Furnace bricks Dynamic random access memories (DRAMs) Chip capacitors
Magnetic	$\gamma\text{-}Fe_2O_3$ $Mn_{0.4}Zn_{0.6}Fe_2O_4$ $BaFe_{12}O_{19}$ $Y_{2.66}Gd_{0.34}Fe_{4.22}Al_{0.68}Mn_{0.09}O_{12}$	Recording tapes Transformer cores in touch tone telephones Permanent magnets in loudspeakers Radar phase shifters
Optical	Doped SiO_2 $a\text{-}Al_2O_3$ Doped $ZrSiO_4$ Doped $(Zn,Cd)S$ $Pb_{1-x}La_x(Zr_zTi_{1-z})_{1-x/4}O_3$ (PLZT) Nd doped $Y_3Al_5O_{12}$	Optical fibers Transparent envelopes in street lamps Ceramic colors Fluorescent screens for electron microscopes Thin-film optical switches Solid-state lasers
Mechanical	TiN SiC Diamond Si_3N_4 Al_2O_3	Wear-resistant coatings Abrasives for polishing Cutting tools Engine components Hip implants
Therma	SiO_2 Al_2O_3 and AlN Lithium-aluminosilicate glass ceramics Pyrex glass	Space shuttle insulation tiles Packages for integrated circuits Supports for telescope mirrors Laboratory glassware and cookware

You may find that in addition to dividing ceramics according to their properties and applications that it is common to class them as *traditional* or *advanced*.

Traditional ceramics include high-volume items such bricks and tiles, toilet bowls (whitewares), and pottery.

Advanced ceramics include newer materials such as laser host materials, piezoelectric ceramics, ceramics for dynamic random access memories (DRAMs), etc., often produced in small quantities with higher prices.

There are other characteristics that separate these categories.

Traditional ceramics are usually based on clay and silica. There is sometimes a tendency to equate traditional ceramics with low technology, however, advanced manufacturing techniques are often used. Competition among producers has caused processing to become more efficient and cost effective. Complex tooling and machinery is often used and may be coupled with computer-assisted process control.

Advanced ceramics are also referred to as "special," "technical," or "engineering" ceramics. They exhibit superior mechanical properties, corrosion/oxidation resistance, or electrical, optical, and/or magnetic properties. While traditional clay-based ceramics have been used for over 25,000 years, advanced ceramics have generally been developed within the last 100 years.

Unit 8   Glass in Building

Introduction

Glass panes are widely used in all modern buildings, commercial or even residential as façade panels or decorative components:

- Aesthetically good-looking
- Varying colors & reflection (coating/film/tinting)
- Different methods of fixing
- Tailored acoustic behavior
- High compressive strength
- Visco-elastic

■ forming into desired shape by heating the glass to the plastic phase to produce complex shapes

■ Sag bending: the glass, supported peripherally and heated to the plastic phase, is allowed to sag under its own weight to the desired shape (gravity sag bending). Control is through the pattern of temperature distribution across the sheet.

■ Between 500-600°C, viscosity falls by a factor of 10,000
■ Glass transforms from a brittle solid to a plastic substance.
- Tailored optical properties (coating or film)
■ Daylight admission
■ Solar gain
■ Opacity
- Surface pattern can be easily introduced
■ Surface patterned
■ Sand blasting and acid etching
■ Surface Printing / Screen Printing

For similar reasons, glass based hardware is also getting very popular in building:
■ washbasins
■ shower screen doors
■ tables & desks
■ cooktops

......

Glass in Building

Float glass: is a term for perfectly flat, clear glass (basic product). The term "float" glass derives from the production method, introduced in the UK by Sir Alastair Pilkington in the late 1950's, by which 90% of today's flat glass is manufactured.

Production: The raw materials (silica sand, calcium, oxide, soda and magnesium) are properly weighted and mixed and then introduced into a furnace where they are melted at 1500° C. The molten glass then flows from the glass furnace into a bath of molten tin in a continuous ribbon. The glass, which is highly viscous, and the tin, which is very fluid, does not mix and the contact surface between these two materials is perfectly flat. When it leaves the bath of molten tin the glass has cooled down sufficiently to pass to an annealing chamber called a lehr. Here it is cooled at controlled temperatures, until it is essentially at room temperature.

Toughened Glass: Toughened glass is two or more times stronger than annealed glass. When broken, it shatters into many small fragments which prevent major injuries. This type of glass is intended for glass façades, sliding doors, building entrances, bath and shower enclosures and other uses requiring superior strength and safety properties.

Production: There are two different methods used to produce tempered glass:

- Heat treating: Where the annealed glass is subjected to a special heat-treatment in which it is heated to about 680°C and afterwards cooled. If it is cooled rapidly, the glass is up to four times stronger then annealed glass and its breaks into many small fragments (fully-tempered). If it is cooled slowly, the glass is twice as strong as annealed glass and the fragments of the broken glass are linear and more likely to remain in the frame (Heat-strengthened).

- Chemical Strengthening: The glass is covered by a chemical solution which produces a higher mechanical resistance. Chemically-strengthened glass has similar properties to thermal-treated glass. The product is not generally used for window glass, but more commonly seen in industries where thin, strong glass is needed.

Coated Glass: Ordinary float glass can be coated to achieve different properties:

Production: Pyrolitic (On-Line): in this process, semi-conducted metal oxides are directly applied to the glass during the float glass production while the glass is still hot in the annealing lehr.

These are hard coatings which are relatively harmful to the environment.

- Vacuum (magnetron) Process (off-line):in this process one or more coats of metal oxide are applied under a vacuum to finished glass. The coatings applied by this technique are soft and must be protected against external influences and are therefore used for the interior side of glass panes.

There are some other techniques for the OFF-LINE coating:

- Immersion Process
- Chemical Process
- Foil

For coated glass, the coating on the glass may be more susceptible to chemical attack:

- Nature of coating (soft or hard)
- Location of coating (outside, inside, between panes)

Strength of Glass

In theory, glass is very strong - much stronger than many metals.

In practice, Glass has very high compressive strength but behaves as a brittle substance (low fracture toughness) with a tensile strength only 0.4 per cent of its theoretical value.

- It is severely weakened by fine cracks caused by abrasions through handling and corrosion by water vapour
- Can be easily damaged by a point load

Heat strengthened and tempered glass in general possesses better fracture toughness, but there exists weak points in these glasses.

The actual load that a glass component could withstand in real service situation is affected by:

- Condition of the glass (amount of pre-existing flaws, edge quality, …)
- Nature of load (impulsive/point or distributed? …)
- Support frame & mounting
- Thermal differential (indoor and outdoor / daily change in temperature …)

Thermal Cracking

All type of glasses is susceptible to thermal cracking

- Lack of allowance for thermal expansion
- Requires proper supports with allowances for expansion

Structural/Shape Stability of Glass

Can a glass pane or component retain its shape after breakage?

- Nature of attack
- Type of support frame and mounting
- Presence of additional load (e.g. Wind loading)
- Type of glass
- Use of Laminated Glass

Laminated Glass:

Laminating procedure:

- Pre-press stage: the laminate is sandwiched between two plates of glass panes and de-aired,
- Autoclaving: the pre-pressed panes are autoclaved under pressure at an elevated temperature.
- Once sealed together, the glass "sandwich" behaves as a single unit and looks like normal glass. Annealed, heat strengthened or tempered glass can be used to produce laminated glass.
- Polyvinyl butyral (PVB) interlayers are commonly used for glass lamination

The toughness and resiliency of laminated glass makes it an excellent safety glazing. If the glass is broken, fragments will adhere to the PVB, reducing the risk of personal injury and property damage

The standard two-ply construction provides resistance to penetration when subjected to attempted force entry. In multi-ply configurations, laminated glass can even resist bullets, heavy objects, or small explosions. In most cases, it takes many blows, all in the same spot, to penetrate the glass.

120

The shear damping performance of the PVB makes laminated glass an effective sound control product.

The PVB in laminated glass helps reduce solar energy transmittance to reduce cooling loads.

The ultraviolet (UV) filtering performance of the plastic interlayer helps protect valuable furnishings, displays or merchandise from the fading effects of UV radiation.

Common Problems

Delamination

The adhesion between the glass and the interlayer was affected by some means

PVB will readily absorb & vaporize water

- During transportation with exposed glass edges or Storage in warehouses without humidity control

- Lowered the adhesive bond strength between the PVB interlayer and the glass

Chemical Damage to PVB laminate:

- Laminate attacked by chemicals, e.g. sealant, this also affects adhesiveness of the laminates

Thermal stresses

- Difference in indoor/outdoor temperature resulting in significant differential movement of the glass panes

- Most pronounce when thickness of indoor/outdoor panes differ significantly (thermal mass)

Trapped air

- Excess air trapped in laminate during production may expand and affect the adhesion of laminate

Residual stresses in laminate

Uneven compression of laminate during the lamination process induced localized residual stresses

Part Ⅳ VOCABULARY

A

abrasion	磨耗，磨损
accelerated test	快速实验
accelerating action	加速所用
accelerator	加速剂
acid attack	酸性侵蚀
acid phospehat	酸式磷酸盐
acrylic fibre	丙烯酸系纤维
acrylonitrile	丙烯腈
activation energy	活化能
activator	激发剂
additive	掺合料
adhesive composition	黏附组分
adipic acid	己二酸
admixture	外加剂
adsor ption complex	吸附络合物
adsorbed water	吸附水
adsorption	吸附
afwillite	硅酸钙石
age effect	龄期影响
ageing	时效
ageing of cement	水泥的时效
aggregate	集料
air content	含气量
air cooled slag	空气冷却矿渣
air detraining agent	消气（泡）剂
air entrainment (includes air void)	引气，引气性（包括气孔）
air viod	气孔
air-entraining admixture	引气外加剂
akermanite	镁黄长石
algae	藻类
alite	阿利特
alkali	碱
alkali aggregate reaction	碱集料反应
alkali attack	碱性侵蚀，碱腐蚀
alkali environment	碱性环境
alkali hydroxide	碱(金属)的氢氧化物
alkali resistance	抗碱性
alkali resistance fibre	抗碱玻璃纤维
alkali silicate	碱金属的硅酸盐

alkyl sulphates	烷基硫酸盐
alternatives	替代物
alumina	氧化铝，矾土
alumina filament	铝丝
aluminum chloride	氯化铝
aluminum oxide hydrate	水化氧化铝
ammonium pentaborate	五硼酸铵
ammonium phosphate	磷酸铵
angular friction	倾斜摩擦
anorthite	钙长石
antifreezing action	防冻作用
antifreezing admixture	防冻外加剂
apparent volume	表观体积
application	应用
aragonite	文石
argillite	泥板岩
artificial stone	人造石
arylsulphonates	芳基磺酸盐
asbestos	石棉
asbestos powder	石棉粉
aspect ratio	长径比
atomic absorption spectropho-tometry	原子吸收光谱
attack	侵蚀
autoclave	蒸压器
autoclaved cement	蒸压水泥
autoclaved product	蒸压制品
azobisisobutyronitril	偶氮二异丁腈

B

bacteria	细菌
bamboo fibre	竹纤维
bamboo pulp	竹纸浆
bangham effect	效应
basalt aggregate	玄武岩集料
bentomite	膨润土
benzene	苯
benzoyl peroxide	过氧化苯酰
biological attack	生物腐蚀
blast furnace slag	高炉矿渣
bleeding	泌水性
blended cement	混合水泥
boiler slag	沸腾炉渣
boiling point, monomer	沸点，单体
bond	黏结，键
bond efficiency factor	有效黏结系数

bond failure	黏结破坏
bond formation	键的形成
bond measurement	黏结测定
bond mechanizm	黏结机理
bond strength	黏结强度
bonding	黏结
bonding, binding	键，结合
borax	硼砂
boric acid	硼酸
borogypsum	硼石膏
borosiliicate glass	鹏硅酸盐玻璃
bridge deck	桥面
brittle fibre	脆性纤维
brittleness	脆性
brucite	水镁石
burnt clay	烧黏土

C

calcite	方解石
calcium aluminate cement	铝酸钙水泥
calcium aluminate hydrate	水化铝酸钙
calcium aluminate-fluorite cement	氟铝酸钙水泥
calcium aluminoferrite	铁铝酸钙
calcium bicarbonate	碳酸氢钙
calcium carbonate	碳酸钙
calcium chloride	氯化钙
calcium chloroaluminate	氯铝酸钙
calcium ferrite	铁酸钙
calcium fluorosilicate	氟硅酸钙
calcium formate	甲酸钙
calcium hydroxid solution method	氢氧化钙溶液法
calcium hydroxide	氢氧化钙
calcium lignosulphonate	木质磺酸钙
calcium nitrate	硝酸钙
calcium silicate	硅酸钙
calcium silicate hydrate	水化硅酸钙
calcium sulphate	硫酸钙
calcium thiosulphate	硫代硫酸钙
calignosulphonate	木质硫酸钙
calorimetric study	热量研究
calorimetry	量热试验
capillary	毛细孔
carbohydrate	碳水化合物
carbohydrate ester	羧水脂
carbon content	含碳量

carbon fibre	碳纤维
carbonate	碳酸盐
carbonated cement	碳化水泥
carbonation	碳（酸）化
carbonation shrinkage	碳化收缩
carbon-reinforced cement	碳纤维增强水泥
carboxylic acid	羧酸
casein	酪素
catalyst	催化剂
cement paste	水泥浆体
cement paste with MgO	含 MgO 水泥浆体
cement-by-product gypsum	水泥-副产品石膏
cementsilica system	水泥-二氧化硅系统
cementsugar free lignosulphonate	水泥-无糖木质硫酸盐
chalcedony	玉髓
chalk	白垩
chemical analysis	化学分析
chemical attack	化学腐蚀，化学侵蚀
chemical method	化学方法
chemical potential	化学位
chemical process	化学过程
chemisorption	化学吸附
chert	黑硅石
chloride	氯化物
chloride penetration	氯化物渗透
chloride free	无氯化物
chloride free accelerator	无氯化物加速剂
chloroaluminate	氯铝酸盐
chloroform	三氯甲烷
chlorostyrene	氯苯乙烯
chromatography	色谱分析
chrysotile	温石棉
citric acid	柠檬酸
classification	分类
clay	黏土
coir	椰纤维
cold joint	冷接
cold weather concreting	混凝土冬季施工
collapse	扁缩，压扁
colliery spoil	煤矸石
colorimetry	比色计
combined efficiency factor	综合有效系数
commercial product	商品
compaction	压实
complex	络合物

composite	复合材料
composition	组成
compressive creep	压缩徐变
compressive strength	抗压强度
concrete	混凝土
concrete under load	荷载下的混凝土
concrete with antifreezing admixture	含防冻剂的混凝土
concrete with water reducer	含减水剂的混凝土
contact angle	接触角
conversion reaction	转化反应
copolymer	共聚物
copper powder	铜粉
copper sulphate	硫酸铜
corrosion	腐蚀，侵蚀，锈蚀
corrosion inhibitor	阻锈剂
corrosion resistance	抗蚀性
corundum	刚玉
cotton fibre	棉纤维
crack	裂缝
crack arrestor	抑制裂缝者
crack length	裂缝长度
crazing	龟裂
creep	徐变
cristobalite	方英石
critical fibre volume	临界纤维容量
critical strain energy	极限应变能
critical stress intesityffactor	临界应力强度因子
crocidolite	青石棉
cross-linking agent	交联剂
cryptocrystalline	陷晶
crystallinity	结晶度
C-S-H structure	C-S-H 结构
curve	曲线
cyclonhexane	环己烷
cylinder	圆柱体

D

dacron	一种聚脂
debonding	脱黏，减黏
dedolomitization	反白云石化
degree of layering	成层程度
degree of hydration(hydration degree)	水化程度
dehydration	脱水
de-icer scaling	除水剂锈蚀
de-icing salt	除冰盐

delayed addition	后掺
density	密度，容重
density relationship	密度关系
dental cement	补齿水泥，牙骨质，牙科黏合剂
desulphogypsum	脱硫石膏
deterioration	破坏
devitrification	反玻璃化
dextrin	糊精
diatomaceous earth	硅藻土
dicalcium silicate	硅酸二钙
dicyclopentadiene	双环戊二烯
differential thermal analysis	差热分析
diffusion	扩散
dimer	二聚物
dimethyl aniline	二甲基苯胺
dimethyl formamide	二甲基甲酸酰胺
dipentene	双戊烷
disc	薄片
discontinuous	不连续的
discontinuous fibre	定长纤维（不连续纤维）
disilicate	二硅酸盐
dispersion	分散
dolomite	白云石
dolomite flux	白云岩助熔矿物
dolomite limestone	白云质石灰岩
dolomite-based	白云石基
dormant period(induction period)	诱导期
dosage	剂量
dowel action	传力作用
drying	干燥
drying shrinkage	干缩
ductivity	延性
durability	耐久性

E

efficiency factor	有效系数
efflorescence	起霜
elastic modulus(modulus of elacticity)	弹性模量
elastic strain energy	弹性应变能
electrode	电极
electron microprobe	电子探针
electron microscope	电子显微镜
elephant glass	象鼻草
elucidation	阐明
embrittlement	变脆

energy adsorption	能量吸收
epoxy	环氧树脂
equation	公式，方程式
estimation	测定
ethyl　acetate	乙酸乙脂
ethyl alcohol(alcohol)	乙醇
ethylene glycol	乙二醇
ettringite	钙矾石
evaporable	蒸发水
evaporable water	可蒸发水
evidence	证据
expansion	膨胀

F

failure mode	破坏方式
fatigue	疲劳
feldman approach	探讨
ferrobacillus	铁杆菌
fibre	纤维
fibre ends	纤维两端
fibre failure	纤维破坏
fibre fracture	纤维断裂
fibre length	纤维长度
fibre matrix misfit	纤维基本不匹配
fibre orientation	纤维取向
fibre spacing	纤维间隙
fibre strength	纤维强度
fibre-cement	纤维水泥
fibre-fibre interaction	纤维-纤维的相互作用
fibre-matrix bond	纤维-基体黏结
fibre-matrix inter face bond	纤维-基体界面黏结
fibre-matrix interface	纤维-基体界面
fibre-reinforced	纤维增强的
fibre-reinforcement	纤维增强
Fick's law	Fick 定律
film	水膜
fire resistance	耐火性
flammability	可燃性
flaw	裂缝，缺陷
flawed	存在缺陷的
flawed fibre	存在缺陷的纤维
flexural creep	弯曲徐变
flexural strength	抗弯强度，抗折强度
flexural stress	弯曲应力
flint	燧石

128

floor heaving	地板隆胀
flowability	流动性
flowing concrete	流态混凝土
fluiding effect	流化效果
fluidity	流动度
fluorate	氟化物
fluorosilicate	氟硅酸盐
fly ash	粉煤灰
fly ash concrete	粉煤灰混凝土
foamed slag	含泡矿渣
formaldehyde	甲醛
formalin	甲醛液
formation	形成
fracture	断裂
fracture energy	断裂能
fracture resisrance	抗裂性
fracture strain	断裂应变
fracture toughness	断裂韧性
fracture work(work of fracture)	断裂功
free energy	自由能
freeze-thaw durability	抗冻融性
freeze-thaw resistance	抗冻融破坏
freezing point	冰点
freezing effect	冻结影响
frictional bond	摩擦黏结
frictional stress	摩擦应力
frictional work	摩擦功
frost action	冻结作用
fructose	果糖
fungi	菌类
furnace bottom ash	炉底灰
furnace clinker	炉熟料

G

galactose	半乳糖
gel	凝胶，凝胶水，胶体
gel permeation chromatography	凝胶渗透色谱分析
gel pore	凝胶孔
gel water	凝胶剂
Gibbs' adsorption	Gibbs 吸附
glass transiton	玻璃化
glass-reinforced cement	玻璃纤维增强水泥
gluconic acid	葡萄糖酸
glycerol	甘油
glyoxal	乙二醛

granulated slag	粒状矿渣
greywacke	杂砂岩
Griffith's theory	Griffith 理论
gypsum	石膏
gypsum by-product	石膏副产品

H

halide	卤化物
heat of hydration	水化热
helium flow	氦流
helium method	氦流法
helium pycnometry	氦比重计法
hemp fibre	大麻纤维
heptonic acid	七酸
hexamethyl disiloxane	六甲基二硅氧烷
high alumina cement	高铝水泥
high range water reducer	高效减水剂
high strength concrete	高强混凝土
Hooke's law	虎克定律
hot pressed cement	热压水泥
hot pressed paste	热压浆体
humidity	湿度
humidity effect	湿度影响
humidity-durability	湿度-耐久性
hydrate	水化物
hydrated cement	水化水泥
hydration	水化
hydration kinetics	水化动力学
hydration product	水化产物
hydraulic radius	水力半径
hydraulicity	水硬性
hydrogen bong	氢键
hydrogen polysulphide	多硫化氢
hydrogen sulphide	硫化氢
hydrophobic	憎水
hydroxycarboxylic acid	羟基羧酸
hydroxylated polymer	羟基化聚合物
hysteresis	滞后

I

ice crystal	冰晶体
illite	伊利石（伊利水云母）
impact strength	抗冲击强度
impregnated body	浸渍体

impregnated porous glass	浸渍多孔玻璃
impregnated system	浸渍系统
improvement	改善
incinerator residue	焚化炉残留物
infrared absorption	红外吸收
infrared spectroscopy	红外光谱
intercalation	层间夹入，渗入
interface	界面
interface bond	界面黏结
interlayer	层间
interlayer space	层间空间
internal	内部的
internal diameter	内半径
internal stress	内应力
interpartical bond	颗粒间键
intrinsic property	固有的本性
iron ore	铁矿
irreversible water	不可逆水
isopropanol	异丙醇
isostere	等重线
isotherm	等温线

J

jarosite	氢氧硫酸钾铁石
Jennite	杰尼特
J-integral	J-积分
jute fibre	黄麻纤维

K

kaolinitic ash	高岭石灰
Kelvar reinforcement	Kelvar 增强
Kevlar fibre	Kevlar 纤维
Kevlar fibre reinforcement	Kevlar 纤维增强

L

larva	幼虫
layering	成层
Le Chatelier boiling test	Le Chatelier 煮沸实验
leaching	浸出
length	长度
length change	长度变化
lightweight aggregate	轻集料
lightweight concrete	轻混凝土
lignosulphonate	木质磺酸盐

lime	石灰	
limestone	石灰石	
lithium compound	锂化合物	
low angle scattering	低角度散射	

M

magnesia	镁砂
magnesite	菱镁矿
magnesium chloride	氯化镁
magnesium hydroxide	氢氧化镁
magnesium oxychloride	氯氧镁
magnesium oxysulphate	氧硫酸镁
magnesium silicate	硅酸镁
magnesium sulphate	硫酸镁
maleic acid	顺丁烯二酸
malic acid	苹果酸
mannose	乳糖
manufacture	生产
map crack	地图状裂缝
marble flour	大理石粉
marine environment	海水环境
measurement	测试
mechanical property	力学性能
mechanizm	机理
melamine formaldehyde	三聚氰胺甲醛
melilite	黄长石
menisci	弯月面
mercury intrusion	压汞
mercury porosimetry	压汞测孔法
metallurgical slag	冶金渣
metglas fibre	金属玻璃纤维
methanol	甲醇
methyl acrylate	丙烯酸甲脂
methyl cellulose	甲基纤维素
methyl cyclopentadiene	甲基环戊二烯
methyl methacrylate	甲基丙烯酸甲酯
mica	云母
mica flakes cement	云母碎片-水泥
mica reinforcement	云母增强
microcrack	微裂缝
micrograph	显微照相
microhardness	显微硬度
micromorphology	微观形貌
microorganism	微生物
microscope	显微镜

132

microsphere	微球
microstructure	微观结构
mildew	霉
mill tailingsr	尾矿
mining and quarrying waste	采矿及采石废料
mixing rule	混合规则,混合律
mixture rule	混合律
modle	模型
modulus	模量
modulus of rupture	抗弯强度
moisture	水分
monocarboaluminate	单碳铝酸盐
monomer	单体
monosulphate	单硫铝酸盐
montmorillonite	蒙脱石
morphology	形貌
mortar bartest	砂浆棱柱体试验
moss	苔藓
Mossbaner spectra	莫斯鲍尔谱
motar bar	砂浆棱柱体
motar bar method	砂浆棱柱体方法
mould	霉菌

N

naphthalene formaldehyde	萘甲醛
neutron activation analysis	中子激活分析
neutron scattering	中子散射
nitrogen	氮
nitrogen adsorption	氮吸附
non-evaporated water	非蒸发水
non-portland cement	非波特兰水泥
nuclear magnetic resonance (NMR)	核磁共振
nucleation	成核作用
nuclei	核
nylon	尼龙

O

oil well	油井
olefinic liquid hydrocarbon	烯族液体 碳水化合物
oligomerization	齐聚
opal	蛋白石
organic solution effect	有机溶液的作用
organogypsum	有机石膏
orientation	取向

orthosilicate	正硅酸盐
osmotic pressure	渗透压
oxalic acid	草酸

P

particle size	颗粒大小
pat test	试饼法试验
periclase	方镁石
permeability	渗透性
pessimum content	最不利含量
petrography	岩相分析
phosphate	磷酸盐
phosphogypsum	磷石膏
phosphoric acid	磷酸
phyllite	千枚岩
pig iron	生铁
plantain fibre	车前草纤维
plasticizer	塑化剂，增塑剂
plasticizing action	塑化作用
pleochroite	多色矿
Poisson's ratio	泊桑比
polymer	聚合物
polymer impregnated concrete	聚合物浸渍混凝土
polymer impregnation	聚合物浸渍
polymer modified cement	聚合物改性水泥
polymerization	聚合
polypropylene	聚丙烯
polysilicate	聚硅酸盐
pore	孔
pore size	孔径
pore structure	孔结构
pore-size distribution	孔径分布
porosimetry	测孔法
porosity	孔隙率
porous body	多孔体
porous glass	多孔玻璃
porous particle	多孔颗粒
portland blast furnace slag cement	波特兰高炉矿渣水泥
portland cement	波特兰水泥
portland cement paste	波特兰水泥浆体
portlandite	氢氧钙石
potassium carbonate	碳酸钾
power station waste	电厂废料
Powers'theory	Powers 理论
pozzolana	火山灰

pozzolanic activity	火山灰活性
pozzolanic cement	火山灰水泥
precast concrete	预制混凝土
prediction of property	性能预测
prestressed cement	预应力水泥
prestressed concrete	预应力混凝土
preventive method	预防措施
prism	棱柱体
process	过程
production from waste	废料产品
promoter	促进剂
property	性能
pulse velocity	脉冲速度
pumice	浮石
pycnometry	比重计法
pyrex glass	pyrex 玻璃
pyrite	黄铁矿
pyrrhotite	硫磺铁矿

Q

quantab method	定量片法
quartz	石英
quasi elastic neutron scattering	准弹性中子散射

R

radiation	辐射
radioactive mineral	放射性矿物
Ramachandran-Feldman theory	R-F 理论
rayon	人造丝
reaction	反应
recycled concrete(reclaimed concrete)	再生混凝土
red mud	赤泥
refractory brick	耐火砖
refractory concrete	耐火混凝土
regulated set	调凝
regulated set cement	调凝水泥,调节水泥
reinforced concrete	钢筋混凝土
reinforcement	增强
relationhip	关系
relative humidity	相对湿度
relaxation time	衰减时间
retardation	延缓作用
retarder	延缓剂
retarder combination	复合缓凝剂

reuss model	reuss 模型
rheology	流变
rice husk	稻壳灰
role	作用

S

saccharide	糖类
salt attack	盐侵蚀
salt gypsum	盐石膏
saw dust	锯木屑
scanning isotherm	巡回等温线
scanning loop	巡回环路
scanning-electron microscope	扫描电镜
seepage	渗出
segregation	离析
semipermeable membrane	半渗透膜
setting	凝结
setting characteristic	凝结性能
setting time	凝结时间
shale	页岩
shear strength	抗剪强度
shear stress	剪切应力
sheet movement	箔叶的运动
shrinkage	收缩
silica	氧化硅
silica flour	石英粉
silica gel	硅胶
silica polymerization	氧化硅聚合
silica tetrahedra	硅氧四面体
silicate	硅酸盐
silico-phosphate cement	硅质磷酸盐水泥
silk acetate	醋酸丝
siloxane	硅氧烷
sisal fibre	剑麻纤维
sisal modulus	剪切模量
slag	矿渣
slate	片石
sludge	污泥浆
slump	坍落度
soapstone flour	皂石粉
soda gypsum	钠石膏
sodium carbonate	碳酸钠
sodium chloride	氯化钠
sodium fluoride	氟化钠
sodium heptonate	庚酸钠

136

sodium hexameta phosphate	六偏磷酸钠
sodium pentachlorophenate	五氯苯钠
sodium phosphate	磷酸钠
sodium sulphate	硫酸钠
sodium tetraborate	四硼酸钠
solid phase	固相
solid solution	固溶体
solid volume	固相体积
soluble alkali	可溶于水的碱
sorel cement	索列尔水泥
sorption	水吸附
soybean flour	豆粉
spacing factor	间隔(隙)系数
specific volume	比体积
specimen	试件
spectrum absorption	光谱吸收
spent oil shale	油页岩渣
spin echo	自旋反射
split cylinder strength	劈裂棱柱体强度
stabilization	稳定化
staining of concrete	混凝土生锈
starch	淀粉
startling's compound	水化钙黄长石化合物
state	状态
steam curing	蒸汽养护
steel fibre	钢纤维
steel reinforcement	钢筋
steel slag	钢渣
stength	强度
stiffness	刚度
stoichiometry	化学成分
strain	应变
strain energy	应变能
stream cured concrete	蒸养混凝土
strength	强度
strength retrogression	强度衰减
stress	应力
stress concentration	应力集中
stress distribution	应力分布
stress transfer	应力传递
structure	结构
styrene	苯乙烯
sucrose	蔗糖
sugar	糖
sugar-free lignosulphonate	无糖木质磺酸盐

sulphale resisting cement	抗硫酸盐水泥
sulphate	硫酸盐
sulphate resistance	抗硫酸盐性
sulphate attack	硫酸盐侵蚀
sulphide	硫化物
sulphonated polymer	磺化聚合物
sulphonic acid ester	磺酸脂
sulphur	硫
sulphur concrete	硫混凝土
sulphur extrusion	硫渗出
sulphur impregnation	硫浸渍
sulphurous acid	亚硫酸
supercooling	过冷
superplasticized concrete	超塑化混凝土
superplasticizer	超塑化剂
supersaturation	过饱和
supersulphated cement	高硫酸盐水泥
surface area	表面积
surface energy	表面能
surface tension	表面张力
swelling	湿胀
Swenson-Sereda theory	Swenson-Sereda 理论

T

tartavic acid	酒石酸
technique	技术
tensile creep	受拉徐变
tensile strain	拉应变
tensile strength	抗拉强度
tensile stress	拉应力
tert-buty lazoisobutyromitrile	特丁基偶氮异丁腈
tert-butyl perbenzoate	特丁基过苯甲脂酸
test	试验
thaumasite	硅灰石膏
thermal method	热分析方法
thermal analysis	热分析
thermal conductivity	导热系数
thermal expansion	热膨胀
thermodynamic	热力学
thermograma	差热图
thermogravimetry	热重分析
thermomechnical analysis	热力学分析
thiobacillus	硫杆菌
thiosulphate	硫代硫酸盐
thoughness	韧性

tile	地砖
time dependence	时间关系
titanogypsum	钛石膏
tobermorite	托勃莫来石
tortuosity	迂回行程
toxic washes	冲刷剂
tremie pipe	导管
tributyl phosphate	三丁基磷酸盐
tricalcium silicate	硅酸三钙
tricresyl phosphate	三甲苯磷酸盐
tridymite	鳞石英
triethanolamine	三乙醇胺
trimer	三聚物
trimethyl borate	三甲基硼酸盐
trimethyl silylation	三甲基甲硅烷
trisodium phosphate	磷酸三钠

U

ultra-rapid hardening cement	超快硬水泥
ultrasonic pulse velocity	超声脉冲速度
unsoundness	体积不安性
urea	尿素

V

Van der Weal's force	范德华力
vaterite	球状方解石
vegetable	植物
vegetable reinforcement	植物纤维增强
vinyl acetate	醋酸乙烯
vinyl chloride	氯乙烯
vinylidine chloride	偏二氯乙烯
viscosity	黏度
vitreous phase	玻璃相
vocanic rock	火山岩
Volhard's method	Volhard 法
volume	体积
volume change	体积变化
volume fraction	体积百分率

W

W/C ratio	水灰比
waste lime sludge	废石灰浆
water penetration	水的渗入
water reduction	减水

water sorption method	水吸附法
water expulsion	水的挤出
water immersion	浸水
water reduced concrete	掺减水剂的混凝土
water reducer	减水剂
water reed	芦苇
water requirement	需水量
water-solid ratio	水固比
weight change	重量变化
weight loss	重量损失
wetting	吸湿
winter concreting	冬季混凝土施工
wollastonite	硅灰石
wood flour	木屑
workability	工作性(度)
wustite	方铁矿

X

xonotlite	硬钙硅石
X-ray diffraction	X 射线衍射
X-ray emission spectroscopy	X 射线发射光谱
X-ray fluorescence	X 射线荧光分析
X-ray scattering	X 射线散射

Y

| Young's modulus | 杨氏模量 |

Z

zeolite	沸石
zeta potential	zeta 电位
zinc lead slag	锌铅渣
zirconia glass	锆质玻璃

140

References

[1] 樊云昌，姜波，等编.建筑材料专业英语. 北京：中国铁道出版社，2002.

[2] 杜永娟主编.无机非金属材料专业英语. 北京：化学工业出版社，2001.

[3] 匡少平主编.材料科学与工程专业英语. 北京：化学工业出版社，2003.

[4] 钱永梅等主编.新编土木工程专业英语. 北京：化学工业出版社，2004.

[5] 郭向荣 陈政清主编. 土木工程专业英语. 北京：中国铁道出版社，2001.

[6] 李嘉 主编. 专业英语（土木工程专业道桥方向）. 北京：人民交通出版社，2003.

[7] 李亚东 主编. 新编土木工程专业英语. 成都：西南交通大学出版社，2000.

[8] 段兵廷 主编. 土木工程专业英语. 湖北：武汉工业大学出版社，2000.

[9] 汪德华 主编. 建筑工程专业英语. 北京：地震出版社，2003.

[10] 王建成等编. 科技英语写作. 西安：西北工业大学出版社，2000.

[11] 邓贤贵 主编. 建筑工程英语（第二版）.武汉：华中理工大学出版社，1997.

[12] Chu-Kia Wang & Charles G. Salmon. Reinforced Concrete Design, New York: Harper International Edition. Harper & ROM Publishers. 1979.

[13] Augustine I. Fredrich. Sons of Martha: Civil Engineering Readings in Modern Literature. New York: ASCE. 1989.

[14] Raymond Sterling, Underground Space Design. Van Nostrand Reinhold, 1993.

[15] Leo Diamant and C. R. Tumblin, Construction Cost Estimates. Second Edition. John Wiley & Sons Inc. 1990.

[16] E. J. Hall. The Language of Civil Engineering in English, 1984.

[17] Edward G. Nawy. Prestressed Concrete, 1989.

[18] Senol Utku. Sc. D etc., Elementary Structural Analysis. Fourth edition, 1991.

[19] Ivor H. Seeley. Civil Engineering Quantities. Fourth edition, 1987.

[20] Jules Houde, Sustainable Development Slowed Down by Bad Construction Practices and Natural and Technological Disasters. Regional Sustainable Development Forums, 1998.